John Irving was born in Exeter, New Hampshire, in 1942, and he once admitted that he was a 'grim' child. Although he excelled in English at school and knew by the time he graduated that he wanted to write novels, it was not until he met a young Southern novelist named John Yount, at the University of New Hampshire, that he received encouragement. 'It was so simple,' he remembers. 'Yount was the first person to point out that anything I did except writing was going to be vaguely unsatisfying.'

In 1963, Irving enrolled at the Institute of European Studies in Vienna, and he later worked as a university lecturer. His first novel, *Setting Free the Bears*, about a plot to release all the animals from the Vienna Zoo, was followed by *The Water Method Man*, an hilarious tale of a man with a complaint more serious than Portnoy's, and *The 158-Pound Marriage*, which exposes the complications of spouse-swapping. Irving achieved international recognition with *The World According to Garp*, which he hoped would 'cause a few smiles among the tough-minded and break a few softer hearts'.

*The Hotel New Hampshire* is a startlingly original family saga, and *The Cider House Rules* is the story of Doctor Wilbur Larch — saint, obstetrician, founder of an orphanage, ether addict and abortionist — and of his favourite orphan, Homer Wells, who is never adopted. John Irving's latest novel, *A Prayer for Owen Meany*, features the most unforgettable character he has yet created.

John Irving has a life-long passion for wrestling, and he plays a wrestling referee in the film of *The World According to Garp*. He now writes full-time, has three children and lives in the United States.

D0064225

# TRYING TO SAVE PIGGY SNEED

John Irving

**BLACK SWAN**

TRYING TO SAVE PIGGY SNEED
A BLACK SWAN BOOK : 0 552 99573 8

Originally published in Great Britain by Bloomsbury Publishing Ltd

PRINTING HISTORY
Bloomsbury edition published 1993
Black Swan edition published 1994

'Trying to Save Piggy Sneed' first appeared in the *New York Times Book
Review* (22 August, 1982).

'Interior Space' first appeared in *Fiction* (Vol. 6, No. 2, 1980).

'Almost in Iowa' first appeared in *Esquire* (November, 1973).

'Weary Kingdom' first appeared in *The Boston Review* (Spring-Summer, 1968).

'Brennbar's Rant' first appeared in *Playboy* (December, 1974).

'Other People's Dreams' first appeared in *Last Night's Stranger – One
Night Stands and Other Staples of Modern Life,* edited by Pat Rotter,
published by A&W publishers (1982, New York).

'The Pension Grillparzer' first appeared in *The World According to Garp,*
first published in the UK by Gollancz (1976).

'The King of the Novel': Introduction copyright © 1986 by Garp Enterprises, Ltd.

Set in 11pt Linotype Melior by
Phoenix Typesetting, Ilkley, West Yorkshire.

Black Swan Books are published by Transworld Publishers Ltd,
61–63 Uxbridge Road, London W5 5SA,
in Australia by Transworld Publishers (Australia) Pty Ltd,
15–25 Helles Avenue, Moorebank, NSW 2170
and in New Zealand by Transworld Publishers (NZ) Ltd,
3 William Pickering Drive, Albany, Auckland.

Reproduced, printed and bound in Great Britain by
Cox & Wyman Ltd, Reading, Berks.

# Contents

# TRYING TO SAVE
# PIGGY SNEED

This is a memoir, but please understand that (to any writer with a good imagination) all memoirs are false. A fiction writer's memory is an especially imperfect provider of detail; we can always imagine a better detail than the one we can remember. The correct detail is rarely, exactly, what happened; the most truthful detail is what *could* have happened, or what *should* have. Half my life is an act of revision; more than half the act is performed with small changes. Being a writer is a strenuous marriage between careful observation and just as carefully imagining the truths you haven't had the opportunity to see. The rest is the necessary, strict toiling with the language; for me this means writing and rewriting the sentences until they sound as spontaneous as good conversation.

With that in mind, I think that I have become a writer because of my grandmother's good manners and – more specifically – because of a retarded garbage collector to whom my grandmother was always polite and kind.

My grandmother is the oldest living English literature

major to have graduated from Wellesley. She lives in an old people's home, now, and her memory is fading; she doesn't remember the garbage collector who helped me become a writer, but she has retained her good manners and her kindness. When other old people wander into her room, by mistake – looking for their own rooms, or perhaps for their previous residences – my grandmother always says, 'Are you lost, dear? Can I help you find where you're *supposed* to be?'

I lived with my grandmother, in her house, until I was almost seven; for this reason my grandmother has always called me 'her boy'. In fact, she never had a boy of her own; she has three daughters. Whenever I have to say goodbye to her now, we both know she might not live for another visit, and she always says, 'Come back soon, dear. You're *my boy*, you know' – insisting, quite properly, that she is more than a grandmother to me.

Despite her being an English literature major, she has not read my work with much pleasure; in fact, she read my first novel and stopped (for life) with that. She disapproved of the language and the subject matter, she told me; from what she's read about the others, she's learned that my language and my subject matter utterly degenerate as my work matures. She's made no effort to read the four novels that followed the first (she and I agree this is for the best). She's very proud of me, she says; I've never probed too deeply concerning *what* she's proud of me *for* – for growing up, at all, perhaps, or just for being 'her boy' – but she's certainly never made me feel uninteresting or unloved.

I grew up on Front Street in Exeter, New Hampshire. When I was a boy, Front Street was lined with elms; it wasn't Dutch elm disease that killed most of them. The two hurricanes that struck back to back, in the fifties,

10

wiped out the elms and strangely modernized the street. First Carol came and weakened their roots; then Edna came and knocked them down. My grandmother used to tease me by saying that she hoped this would contribute to my respect for women.

When I was a boy, Front Street was a dark, cool street – even in the summer – and none of the backyards was fenced; everyone's dog ran free, and got into trouble. A man named Poggio delivered groceries to my grandmother's house. A man named Strout delivered the ice for the icebox (my grandmother resisted refrigerators until the very end). Mr Strout was unpopular with the neighborhood dogs – perhaps because he would go after them with the ice tongs. We children of Front Street never bothered Mr Poggio, because he used to let us hang around his store – and he was liberal with treats. We never bothered Mr Strout either (because of his ice tongs and his fabulous aggression towards dogs, which we could easily imagine being turned towards us). But the garbage collector had nothing for us – no treats, no aggression – and so we children reserved our capacity for teasing and taunting (and otherwise making trouble) for him.

His name was Piggy Sneed. He smelled worse than any man I *ever* smelled – with the possible exception of a dead man I caught the scent of, once, in Istanbul. And you would have to be dead to look worse than Piggy Sneed looked to us children on Front Street. There were so many reasons for calling him 'Piggy', I wonder why one of us didn't think of a more original name. To begin with, he lived on a pig farm. He raised pigs, he slaughtered pigs; more importantly, he lived *with* his pigs – it was *just* a pig farm, there was no farm house, there was *only* the barn. There was a

11

single stovepipe running into one of the stalls. That stall was heated by a wood stove for Piggy Sneed's comfort – and, we children imagined, his pigs (in the winter) would crowd around him for warmth. He certainly smelled that way.

Also he had absorbed, by the uniqueness of his retardation and by his proximity to his animal friends, certain piglike expressions and gestures. His face would jut in front of his body when he approached the garbage cans, as if he were rooting (hungrily) underground; he squinted his small, red eyes; his nose twitched with all the vigor of a snout; there were deep pink wrinkles on the back of his neck – and the pale bristles, which sprouted at random along his jawline, in no way resembled a beard. He was short, heavy, and strong – he *heaved* the garbage cans to his back, he *hurled* their contents into the wooden, slat-sided truck bed. In the truck, ever eager to receive the garbage, there were always a few pigs. Perhaps he took different pigs with him on different days; perhaps it was a treat for them – they didn't have to wait to eat the garbage until Piggy Sneed drove it home. He took *only* garbage – no paper, plastic, or metal trash – and it was *all* for his pigs. This was all he did; he had a very exclusive line of work. He was paid to pick up garbage, which he fed to his pigs. When *he* got hungry (we imagined), he ate a pig. 'A whole pig, at once', we used to say on Front Street. But the *piggiest* thing about him was that he couldn't talk. His retardation either had deprived him of his human speech or had deprived him, earlier, of the ability to learn human speech. Piggy Sneed didn't talk. He grunted. He squealed. He *oinked* – that was his language; he learned it from his friends, as we learn ours.

12

We children, on Front Street, would sneak up on him when he was raining the garbage down on his pigs – we'd surprise him: from behind hedges, from under porches, from behind parked cars, from out of garages and cellar bulkheads. We'd leap out at him (we never got too close) and we'd squeal at him: 'Piggy! Piggy! Piggy! Piggy! OINK! WEEEE!' And, like a pig – panicked, lurching at random, mindlessly startled *(every time* he was startled, as if he had no memory) – Piggy Sneed would squeal back at us as if we'd stuck him with the slaughtering knife, he'd bellow OINK! out at us as if he'd caught us trying to bleed him in his sleep.

I can't imitate his sound; it was awful, it made all us Front Street children scream and run and hide. When the terror passed, we couldn't wait for him to come again. He came twice a week. What a luxury! And every week or so my grandmother would pay him. She'd come out to the back where his truck was – where we'd often just startled him and left him snorting – and she'd say, 'Good day, Mr Sneed!'

Piggy Sneed would become instantly childlike – falsely busy, painfully shy, excruciatingly awkward. Once he hid his face in his hands, but his hands were covered with coffee grounds; once he crossed his legs so suddenly, while he tried to turn his face away from Grandmother, that he fell down at her feet.

'It's nice to see you, Mr Sneed,' Grandmother would say – not flinching, not in the slightest, from his stench. 'I hope the children aren't being rude to you,' she'd say. 'You don't have to tolerate any rudeness from them, you know,' she would add. And then she'd pay him his money and peer through the wooden slats of the truck bed, where his pigs were savagely attacking the

13

new garbage – and, occasionally, each other – and she'd say, 'What beautiful pigs these are! Are these your *own* pigs, Mr Sneed? Are they *new* pigs? Are these the same pigs as the other week?' But despite her enthusiasm for his pigs, she could never entice Piggy Sneed to answer her. He would stumble, and trip, and twist his way around her, barely able to contain his pleasure: that my grandmother clearly approved of his pigs, that she even appeared to approve (wholeheartedly!) of *him*. He would grunt softly to her.

When she'd go back in the house, of course – when Piggy Sneed would begin to back his ripe truck out the driveway – we Front Street children would surprise him again, popping up on both sides of the truck, making both Piggy and his pigs squeal in alarm, and snort with protective rage.

'Piggy! Piggy! Piggy! Piggy! OINK! WEEE!'

He lived in Stratham – on a road out of our town that ran to the ocean, about eight miles away. I moved (with my father and mother) out of Grandmother's house (before I was seven, as I told you). Because my father was a teacher, we moved into academy housing – Exeter was an all-boys' school, then – and so our garbage (together with our nonorganic trash) was picked up by the school.

Now I would like to say that I grew older and realized (with regret) the cruelty of children, and that I joined some civic organization dedicated to caring for people like Piggy Sneed. I can't claim that. The code of small towns is simple but encompassing: if many forms of craziness are allowed, many forms of cruelty are ignored. Piggy Sneed was tolerated; he went on being himself, living like a pig. He was tolerated as a harmless

14

animal is tolerated – by children, he was indulged; he was even encouraged to be a pig.

Of course, growing older, we Front Street children knew that he was retarded – and gradually we learned that he drank a bit. The slat-sided truck, reeking of pig, of waste, or *worse* than waste, careened through town all the years I was growing up. It was permitted, it was given room to spill over – en route to Stratham. Now there was a town, Stratham! In small-town life is there anything more provincial than the tendency to sneer at *smaller* towns? Stratham was not Exeter (not that Exeter was much).

In Robertson Davies's novel *Fifth Business,* he writes about the townspeople of Deptford: 'We were serious people, missing nothing in our community and feeling ourselves in no way inferior to larger places. We did, however, look with pitying amusement on Bowles Corners, four miles distant and with a population of one hundred and fifty. To live in Bowles Corners, we felt, was to be rustic beyond redemption.'

Stratham was Bowles Corners to us Front Street children – it was 'rustic beyond redemption'. When I was fifteen, and began my association with the academy – where there were students from abroad, from New York, even from California – I felt so superior to Stratham that it surprises me, now, that I joined the Stratham Volunteer Fire Department; I don't remember *how* I joined. I think I remember that there was no Exeter Volunteer Fire Department; Exeter had the other kind of fire department, I guess. There were several Exeter residents – apparently in need of something to volunteer *for*? – who joined the Stratham Volunteers. Perhaps our contempt for the people of Stratham was so vast that we believed they could not even be relied upon to properly put out their own fires.

There was also an undeniable thrill, midst the routine rigors of prep-school life, to be a part of something that could call upon one's services without the slightest warning: that burglar alarm in the heart, which is the late-night ringing telephone – that call to danger, like a doctor's beeper shocking the orderly solitude and safety of the squash court. It made us Front Street children important; and, as we grew only slightly older, it gave us a status that only disasters can create for the young.

In my years as a firefighter, I never rescued anyone – I never even rescued anyone's pet. I never inhaled smoke, I never suffered a burn, I never saw a soul fall beyond the reach of the safety bag. Forest fires are the worst and I was only in one, and only on the periphery. My only injury – 'in action' – was caused by a fellow firefighter throwing his Indian pump into a storage room where I was trying to locate my baseball cap. The pump hit me in the face and I had a bloody nose for about three minutes.

There were occasional fires of some magnitude at Hampton Beach (one night an unemployed saxophone player, reportedly wearing a pink tuxedo, tried to burn down the casino), but we were always called to the big fires as the last measure. When there was an eight- or ten-alarm fire, Stratham seemed to be called last; it was more an invitation to the spectacle than a call to arms. And the local fires in Stratham were either mistakes or lost causes. One night Mr Skully, the meter reader, set his station wagon on fire by pouring vodka in the carburetor – because, he said, the car wouldn't start. One night Grant's dairy barn was ablaze, but all the cows – and even most of the hay – had been rescued

16

before we arrived. There was nothing to do but let the barn burn, and hose it down so that cinders from it wouldn't catch the adjacent farm house on fire.

But the boots, the heavy hard hat (with your own number), the glossy black slicker – *your own ax!* – these were pleasures because they represented a kind of adult responsibility in a world where we were considered (still) too young to drink. And one night, when I was sixteen, I rode a hook-and-ladder truck out the coast road, chasing down a fire in a summer house near the beach (which turned out to be the result of children detonating a lawn mower with barbecue fluid), and there – weaving on the road in his stinking pick-up, blocking our importance, as independent of civic responsibility (or any other kind) as any pig – was a drunk-driving Piggy Sneed, heading home with his garbage for his big-eating friends.

We gave him the lights, we gave him the siren – I wonder, now, what he thought was behind him. God, the red-eyed screaming monster over Piggy Sneed's shoulder – the great robot pig of the universe and outer space! Poor Piggy Sneed, near home, so drunk and foul as to be barely human, veered off the road to let us pass, and as we overtook him – we Front Street children – I distinctly heard us calling, 'Piggy! Piggy! Piggy! Piggy! OINK! WEEEE!' I suppose I heard my voice, too.

Clinging to the hook-and-ladder, our heads thrown back so that the trees above the narrow road appeared to veil the stars with a black, moving lace – the pig smell faded to the raw, fuel-burning stink of the sabotaged lawn mower, which faded finally to the clean salt wind off the sea.

In the dark, driving back, past the pig barn, we noted the surprisingly warm glow from the kerosene lamp in

17

Piggy Sneed's stall. He had gotten safely home. And was he up, reading? we wondered. And once again I heard our grunts, our squeals, our oinks – our strictly animal communication with him.

The night his pig barn burned, we were so surprised.

The Stratham Volunteers were used to thinking of Piggy Sneed's place as a necessary, reeking ruin on the road between Exeter and the beach – a foul-smelling landmark on warm summer evenings, passing it always engendered the obligatory groans. In winter, the smoke from the wood stove pumped regularly from the pipe above Piggy's stall, and from the outdoor pens, stamping routinely in a wallow of beshitted snow, his pigs breathed in little puffs as if they were furnaces of flesh. A blast from the siren could scatter them. At night coming home, when whatever fire there was was out, we couldn't resist hitting the siren as we passed by Piggy Sneed's place. It was too exciting to imagine the damage done by that sound: the panic among the pigs, Piggy himself in a panic, all of them hipping up to each other with their wheezy squeals, seeking the protection of the herd.

That night Piggy Sneed's place burned, we Front Street children were imagining a larkish, if somewhat retarded, spectacle. Out the coast road, lights up full and flashing, siren up high – driving all those pigs crazy – we were in high spirits, telling lots of pig jokes: about how we imagined the fire was started, how they'd been having a drinking party, Piggy *and* his pigs, and Piggy was cooking one (on a spit) and dancing with another one, and some pig backed into the wood stove and burned his tail, knocked over the bar, and the pig that Piggy danced with *most* nights was ill-humored because Piggy *wasn't* dancing with *her* . . . but then we arrived, and we saw that this fire wasn't a party; it wasn't even the tail end of a bad party. It was the biggest fire that we Front Street children, and even the veterans among the Stratham Volunteers, had ever seen.

The low, adjoining sheds of the pig barn appeared to have burst, or melted their tin roofs. There was nothing in the barn that wouldn't burn – there was wood for the wood stove, there was hay, there were eighteen pigs and Piggy Sneed. There was all that kerosene. Most of the stalls in the pig barn were a couple of feet deep in manure, too. As one of the veterans of the Stratham Volunteers told me, 'You get it hot enough, even shit will burn.'

It was hot enough. We had to move the fire trucks down the road; we were afraid the new paint, or the new tires, would blister in the heat. 'No point in wasting the water,' our captain told us. We sprayed the trees across the road; we sprayed the woods beyond the pig barn. It was a windless, bitter cold night, the snow as dry and fine as talcum powder. The trees drooped with icicles and cracked as soon as we sprayed them. The captain decided to let the fire burn itself out; there would be less of a mess that way. It might be dramatic to say that we heard squeals, to say that we heard the pigs' intestines swelling and exploding – or before that, their hooves hammering on the stall doors. But by the time we arrived, those sounds were over; they were history; we could only imagine them.

This is a writer's lesson: to learn that the sounds we imagine can be the clearest, loudest sounds of all. By the time we arrived, even the tires on Piggy's truck had burst, the gas tank had exploded, the windshield had caved in. Since we hadn't been present

19

for those events, we could only guess at the order in which they had taken place.

If you stood too close to the pig barn, the heat curled your eyelashes – the fluid under your eyelids felt searing hot. If you stood too far back, the chill of the winter night air, drawn toward the flames, would cut through you. The coast road iced over, because of spillage from our hoses, and (about midnight) a man with a Texaco emblem on his cap and parka skidded off the road and needed assistance. He was drunk and was with a woman who looked much too young for him – or perhaps it was his daughter. 'Piggy!' the Texaco man hollered. 'Piggy!' he called, into the blaze. 'If you're in there, Piggy – you *moron* – you better get the hell out!'

The only other sound, until about two in the morning, was the occasional *twang* from the tin roof contorting – as it writhed free of the barn. About two the roof fell in; it made a whispering noise. By three there were no walls standing. The surrounding, melted snow had formed a lake that seemed to be rising on all sides of the fire, almost reaching the level of heaped coals. As more snow melted, the fire was being extinguished from underneath itself.

And what did we smell? That cooked-barnyard smell of mid-summer, the conflicting rankness of ashes in snow, the determined baking of manure – the imagination of bacon, or roast pork. Since there was no wind, and we weren't trying to put the fire out, we suffered no smoke abuse. The men (that is to say, the veterans) left us boys to watch after things for an hour before dawn. That is what men do when they share work with boys: they do what they want to do, they have the boys tend to what they don't want to tend to. The

men went out for coffee, they said, but they came back
smelling of beer. By then the fire was low enough to
be doused down. The men initiated this procedure;
when they tired of it, they turned it over to us boys.
The men went off again, at first light – for breakfast,
they said. In the light I could recognize a few of my
comrades, the Front Street children.

With the men away, one of the Front Street children
started it – at first, very softly. It may have been me.
'Piggy, Piggy,' one of us called. One reason I'm a writer
is that I sympathized with our need to do this; I have
never been interested in what nonwriters call good and
bad 'taste'.

'Piggy! Piggy! Piggy! Piggy! OINK! WEEEE!' we
called. That was when I understood that comedy was
just another form of condolence. And then I started it;
I began my first story.

'Shit,' I said – because everyone in the Stratham
Volunteers began every sentence with the word 'shit'.

'Shit,' I said. 'Piggy Sneed isn't in there. He's crazy,'
I added, 'but nobody's that stupid.'

'His truck's there,' said one of the least imaginative
of the Front Street children.

'He just got sick of pigs,' I said. 'He left town, I
know it. He was sick of the whole thing. He probably planned this – for weeks.'

Miraculously, I had their attention. Admittedly, it
had been a long night. *Anyone* with almost *anything*
to say might have easily captured the attention of the
Stratham Volunteers. But I felt the thrill of a rescue
coming – my first.

'I bet there's not a pig in there, either,' I said. 'I bet
he ate half of them – in just a few days. You know,
he stuffed himself! And then he sold the rest. He's

been putting some money away, for precisely this occasion.'

'For *what* occasion?' some skeptic asked me. 'If Piggy isn't in there, where is he?'

'If he's been out all night,' another said, 'then he's *frozen* to death.'

'He's in Florida,' I said. 'He's retired.' I said it just that simply – I said it as if it were a *fact*. 'Look around you!' I shouted to them. 'What's he been spending his money on? He's saved a bundle. He set fire to his own place,' I said, 'just to give us a hard time. Think of the hard time we gave him,' I said, and I could see everyone thinking about that; that was, at least, the truth. A little truth never hurt a story. 'Well,' I concluded. 'He's paid us back – that's clear. He's kept us standing around all night.'

This made us Front Street children thoughtful, and in that thoughtful moment I started my first act of revision; I tried to make the story better, and more believable. It was essential to rescue Piggy Sneed, of course, but what would a man who couldn't talk do in *Florida*? I imagined they had tougher zoning laws than we had in New Hampshire – especially regarding pigs.

'You know,' I said, 'I bet he *could* talk – all the time. He's probably *European*,' I decided. 'I mean, what kind of name is *Sneed*? And he first appeared here around the war, didn't he? Whatever his native language is, anyway, I bet he speaks it pretty well. He just never learned *ours*. Somehow, pigs were easier. Maybe *friendlier*,' I added thinking of us all. 'And now he's saved up enough to go home. That's where he is!' I said. 'Not Florida – he's gone back to *Europe*!'

''Atta boy, Piggy,' someone cheered.

'Look out, Europe,' someone said, facetiously.

Enviously, we imagined how Piggy Sneed had gotten 'out' – how he'd escaped the harrowing small-town loneliness (and fantasies) that threatened us all. But when the men came back, I was confronted with the general public's dubious regard for fiction.

'Irving thinks Piggy Sneed is in Europe,' one of the Front Street boys told the captain.

'He first appeared here around the war, didn't he, sir?' I asked the captain, who was staring at me as if I were the first *body* to be recovered from this fire.

'Piggy Sneed was *born* here, Irving,' the captain told me. 'His mother was a half-wit, she got hit by a car going the wrong way around the bandstand. Piggy was born on Water Street,' the captain told us. Water Street, I knew perfectly well, ran into Front Street – quite close to home.

So, I thought, Piggy was in Florida, after all. In stories, you must make the best thing that *can* happen happen (or the worst, if that is your aim), but it still has to ring true.

When the coals were cool enough to walk on, the men started looking for him; discovery was a job for the men – it being more interesting than waiting, which was boys' work.

After a while, the captain called me over to him. 'Irving,' he said. 'Since you think Piggy Sneed is in Europe, then you won't mind taking whatever *this* is out of here.'

It required little effort, the removal of this shrunken cinder of a man; I doused down a tarp and dragged the body, which was extraordinarily light, on to the tarp with first the long and then the short gaff. We found all eighteen of his pigs, too. But even today I can imagine him more vividly in Florida than I can imagine him existing in that impossibly small shape of charcoal I extricated from the ashes.

Of course I told my grandmother the *plain* truth, just the boring facts. 'Piggy Sneed died in that fire last night, Nana,' I told her.

'Poor Mr Sneed,' she said. With great wonder, and sympathy, she added: 'What awful circumstances forced him to live such a savage life!'

What I would realize, later, is that the writer's business is *both* to imagine the possible rescue of Piggy Sneed *and* to set the fire that will trap him. It was *much* later – but before my grandmother was moved to the old people's home, when she still remembered who Piggy Sneed was – when Grandmother asked me, 'Why, in heaven's name, have you become a *writer*?'

I was 'her boy,' as I've told you, and she was sincerely worried about me. Perhaps being an English literature major had convinced her that being a writer was a lawless and destructive thing to be. And so I told her everything about the night of the fire, about how I imagined that if I could have invented well enough – if I could have made up something truthful enough – that I could have (in some sense) saved Piggy Sneed. At least saved him for another fire – of my own making.

Well, my grandmother is a Yankee – *and* Wellesley's oldest living English literature major. Fancy answers, especially of an aesthetic nature, are not for her. Her late husband – my grandfather – was in the shoe business; he made things people really needed: practical protection for their feet. Even so, I insisted to Grandmother that her kindness to Piggy Sneed had not been overlooked by me – and that this, in combination with the helplessness of Piggy Sneed's special human

24

condition, and the night of the fire, which had introduced me to the possible power of my own imagination . . . and so forth. My grandmother cut me off.

With more pity than vexation, she patted my hand, she shook her head. 'Johnny, *dear,'* she said. 'You surely could have saved yourself a lot of *bother,* if you'd only treated Mr Sneed with a little human decency when he was alive.'

Failing that, I realize that a writer's business is setting fire to Piggy Sneed – *and* trying to save him – again and again; forever.

# INTERIOR SPACE

George Ronkers was a young urologist in a university town – a lucrative situation nowadays; the uninformed liberality of both the young and old college community produced a marvel of venereal variety. A urologist had plenty to do. Ronkers was affectionately nicknamed by a plethora of his clientele at Student Health. 'Raunchy Ronk,' they said. With deeper affection, his wife called him 'Raunch'.

Her name was Kit; she had a good sense of humor about George's work and a gift for imaginative shelter. She was a graduate student in the School of Architecture; she had a Teaching Assistantship, and she taught one course to undergraduate architecture students called 'Interior Space'.

It was her field, really. She was completely responsible for all the interior space in the Ronkers home. She had knocked down walls, sunk bathtubs, arched doorways, rounded rooms, ovalled windows; in short, she treated interior space as an illusion. 'The trick,' she would say, 'is not letting you see where one room ends and another begins; the concept of a *room* is defeating to the concept of *space*; you can't make out the boundaries . . .' And so on; it was her field.

George Ronkers walked through his house as if it were a park in a foreign but intriguing city. Theories of space didn't bother him one way or another.

'Saw a girl today with seventy-five warts,' he'd say. 'Really an obvious surgery. Don't know why she came to *me*. Really should have seen a *gynecologist* first.'

The only part of the property that Ronkers considered *his* field was the large, lovely black walnut tree beside the house. Kit had spotted the house first; it belonged to an old Austrian named Kesler whose wife had just died. Kit told Ronkers it was repairable inside because the ceilings were at least high enough. But Ronkers had been sold on account of the tree. It was a split-trunked black walnut, growing out of the ground like two trees, making a high, slim V. The proper black walnut has a tall, graceful, upshooting style – the branches and the leaves start about two stories off the ground, and the leaves are small, slender, and clustered very closely together; they are a delicate green, turning yellow in October. The walnuts grow in a tough rubbery pale-green skin; in the fall they reach the size of peaches; the skins begin to darken – even blackening in spots – and they start to drop. Squirrels like them.

Kit liked the tree well enough, but she was ecstatic telling old Herr Kesler what she was going to do with his house after he moved out. Kesler just stared at her, saying, occasionally, 'Which wall? *That* wall? You're going *this* wall to down-take, yes? Oh, the *other* wall too? Oh. Well . . . what will the ceiling up-hold? Oh . . .'

And Ronkers told Kesler how *much* he liked the

30

black walnut tree. That was when Kesler warned him about their neighbor.

'*Der Bardlong,*' Kesler said. 'He wants the tree down-chopped but I never to him listened.' George Ronkers tried to press old Kesler to explain the motives of his would-be neighbor Bardlong, but the Austrian suddenly thumped the wall next to him with the flat of his hand and cried to Kit, 'Not *this* wall too, I hope not! Ah, this wall I always *enjoyed* have!'

Well, they had to be delicate. No more plans out loud until Kesler moved out. He moved to an apartment in another suburb; for some reason, he dressed for the occasion – like a Tyrolean peasant, his felt Alpine hat with a feather in it and his old white knees winking under his lederhosen, he stood in a soft spring rain by his ancient wooden trunks and let George and Kit hustle the furniture around for him.

'Won't you get out of the rain, Mr Kesler?' Kit asked him, but he would not budge from the sidewalk in front of his former house until all his furniture was in the truck. He was watching the black walnut tree.

Herr Kesler put his hand frankly on Kit's behind, saying to her, 'Do not let *der pest Bardlong* the tree down-chop, okay?'

'Okay,' said Kit.

George Ronkers liked to lie in bed in the spring mornings and watch the sun filter through the new green leaves of his black walnut tree. The patterns the tree cast on the bed were almost mosaic. Kit had enlarged the window to accommodate more of the tree; her term for it was 'inviting the tree in'.

'Oh, Raunch,' she whispered, 'isn't it lovely?'

'It's a lovely tree.'

'Well, I mean the *room* too. And the window, the elevated sleeping platform . . .'

'*Platform?* I thought it was a bed.'

There was a squirrel who came along a branch very near the window – in fact, he often brushed the screen with his tail; the squirrel liked to tug at the new nuts, as if he could anticipate autumn.

'Raunch?'

'Yup . . .'

'Remember the girl with seventy-five warts?'

'*Remember* her!'

'Well, Raunch . . . *where* were the warts?'

. . . and *der pest Bardlong* gave them no trouble. All that spring and hot summer, when workmen were removing walls and sculpting windows, the aloof Mr and Mrs Bardlong smiled at the confusion from their immaculate grounds, waved distantly from their terraces, made sudden appearances from behind a trellis – but always they were neighborly, encouraging of the youthful bustle, prying into nothing.

Bardlong was retired. He was *the* Bardlong, if you're at all familiar with the shock absorber and brake systems magnate. In the Midwest, you maybe have seen the big trucks.

BARDLONG STOPS YOU SHORT!
BARDLONG TAKES THAT SHOCK!

Even in retirement, Bardlong appeared to be absorbing whatever shock his new neighbors and their renovations might have caused him. His own house was an old red-brick mansion, trimmed tastefully with dark green shutters and overcrawling with ivy. It imitated a Georgian version of architecture; the front of the house was square and centered with tall, thin downstairs windows. The depth of the house was considerable; it went back a long way, branching into terraces, trellises, rock gardens, manicured hedges, fussed-over flower beds, and a lawn as fine as a putting green.

The house took up a full corner of the shady, suburban street. Its only neighbor was the Ronkers' house, and the Bardlongs' property was walled off from George and Kit by a low slate-stone wall. From their second-floor windows, George and Kit looked down into Bardlong's perfect yard; their tangle of bushes and unkempt, matted grass was a full five feet above the apparent dike which kept their whole mess from crushing Bardlong as he raked and pruned. The houses themselves were queerly close together, the Ronkers' having once been servant quarters to the Bardlongs', long before the property was divided.

Between them, rooted on the raised ground on Ronkers' side of the slate-stone wall, was the black walnut tree. Ronkers could not imagine whatever had prodded old Herr Kesler to think that Bardlong wanted the demise of the tree. Perhaps it had been a language problem. The tree must have been a shared joy to Bardlong. It shaded *his* windows, too; its stately height towered over his roof. One veer of the V angled over George and Kit; the other part of the V leaned over Bardlong.

Did the man not care for unpruned beauty?

Possibly; but all summer long, Bardlong never complained. He was there in his faded straw hat gardening, simply puttering, often accompanied by his wife. The two of them seemed more like guests in an elegant old resort hotel than actual residents. Their dress, for yard work, was absurdly formal – as if Bardlong's many years as a brake systems businessman had left him with no clothes other than business suits. He wore slightly out-of-style suit trousers, with suspenders, and slightly out-of-style dress shirts – the wide-brimmed straw hat shading his pale, freckled forehead. He was complete with an excessively sporty selection of two-toned shoes.

His wife – in a lawn-party dress and a cream-white Panama with a red silk ribbon round the bun at the back of her nail-gray hair – tapped her cane at bricks in the terrace which might dare to be loose. Bardlong followed her with a tiny, toylike pull-cart of cement, and a trowel.

They lunched every midafternoon under a large sun umbrella on their back terrace, the white iron lawn furniture gleaming from an era of hunt breakfasts and champagne brunches following a daughter's wedding.

A visit of grown-up children and less grown-up grandchildren seemed to mark the only interruption to Bardlong's summer. Three days of a dog barking and of balls being tossed about the pool-table symmetry of that yard seemed to upset the Bardlongs for a week following. They anxiously trailed the children around the grounds, trying to mend broken stalks of flowers, spearing on some garden instrument the affront of a gum wrapper, replacing divots dug up by the wild-running dog who could, and had, cut like a halfback through the soft grass.

For a week after this family invasion, the Bardlongs were collapsed on the terrace under their sun umbrella, too tired to tap a single brick or repair a tiny torn arm of ivy ripped from a trellis by a passing child.

'Hey, Raunch,' Kit whispered. 'Bardlong takes that shock!'

'Bardlong stops you short!' Ronkers would read off the trucks around town. But never did one of those crude vehicles so much as approach the fresh-painted curb by Bardlong's house. Bardlong was, indeed, retired. And the Ronkers found it impossible to imagine the man as ever having lived another way. Even when his daily fare had been brake systems and shock absorbers, the Ronkers couldn't conceive of Bardlong having taken part.

George once had a daydream of perverse exaggeration. He told Kit he had watched a huge BARDLONG STOPS YOU SHORT! truck dump its entire supply in Bardlong's yard – the truck with its big back-panel doors flung wide open, churning up the lawn and disgorging itself of clanking parts: brake drums and brake shoes and great oily slicks of brake fluid, rubbery, springing shock absorbers mashing down the flower beds.

'Raunch?' Kit whispered.

'Yup . . .'

'Were the warts actually *in* her vagina?'

'In it, on it, all around it . . .'

*'Seventy-five!* Oh Raunch, I can't imagine it.'

They lay in bed dappled by the late summer sun, which in the early morning could scarcely penetrate the thick weave of leaves fanned over their window by the black walnut tree.

'You know what I love about lying here?' Ronkers asked his wife. She snuggled up to him.

'Oh no, tell . . .'

'Well, it's the *tree,*' he said. 'I think my first sexual experience was in a tree house and that's what it's like up here . . .'

'You and the damn tree,' Kit said. 'It might be my

35

*architecture* that makes you like that tree so much. Or even *me,'* she said. 'And *that's* a likely story – I can't imagine you doing it in a tree house, frankly – that sounds like something one of your dirty old patients told you . . .'

'Well, actually it was a dirty *young* one.'

'You're awful, Raunch. My God, seventy-five *warts* . . .'

'Quite a lot of surgery for such a spot, too.'

'I thought you said Tomlinson did it.'

'Well, yes, but I *assisted*.'

'You don't *normally* do that, do you?'

'Well, no, but this wasn't *normal*.'

'You're really awful, Raunch . . .'

'Purely medical interest, professional desire to learn. You use a lot of mineral oil and twenty-five percent podophyllin. The cautery is delicate . . .'

'Turds,' Kit said.


But summer soon ends, and with the students back in town Ronkers was too busy to lie long abed in the mornings. There is a staggering host of urinary tract infections to be discovered in all corners of the globe, a little-known fringe benefit of the tourist trade; perhaps it is the nation's largest unknown summer import.

A line of students waited to see him each morning, their summer travel ended, their work begun in earnest, their peeing problems growing more severe.

'Doc, I think I picked this up in Izmir.'

'The question is, how much has it gotten around *since*?'

'The trouble', Ronkers told Kit, 'is that they all know perfectly well, at the first sign, what it is they've got – and, usually, even from *whom*. But almost all of them spend some time waiting for it to go away – or passing it on, for Christ's sake! – and they don't come to me until they can't *stand* it any more.'

But Ronkers was very sympathetic to his venereal patients and did not make them feel steeped in sin or wallowing in their just rewards; he said they should not feel guilty for catching anything from absolutely anybody. However, he was tough about insisting that they inform the original hostess – whenever they knew her. 'She may not *know*,' Ronkers would say.

'We are no longer communicating,' they'd say.

And Ronkers would charge, 'Well, she's just going to be passing it on to someone else, who in turn . . .'

'Good for them!' they'd holler.

'No, *look*,' Ronkers would plead. 'It's more serious than that, for *her*.'

'Then *you* tell her,' they'd say. 'I'll give you her number.'

'Oh, *Raunch*!' Kit would scream. 'Why don't you make *them* do it?'

'How?' Ronkers would ask.

'Tell them you won't *fix* them. Tell them you'll let them pee themselves *blind*!'

'They'd just go to someone else,' Ronkers would say. 'Or they'd simply tell me that they've already told the person – when they haven't, and never intend to.'

'Well, it's absurd, *you* calling up every other woman in the damn town.'

'I just hate the long-distance ones,' Ronkers would say.

'Well, you can at least make *them* pay for the calls, Raunch!'

'Some of these students don't have any money.'

'Tell them you'll ask their *parents* to pay, then!'

'It's tax-deductible, Kit. And they're not all students, either.'

'It's awful, Raunch. It really *is*.'

'How much higher are you going to make this damn sleeping platform?'

'I like to make you work for it, Raunch.'

'I know, but a *ladder,* my God . . .'

'Well, it's up in your favorite tree, right? And you like that, I'm told. And anyone who gets me has got to be athletic.'

'I may get maimed trying.'

'Raunch! Who are you calling *now*?'

'Hello?' he said to the phone. 'Hello, is this Miss Wentworth? Oh, *Mrs* Wentworth, well . . . I guess I would like to speak to your *daughter,* Mrs Wentworth. Oh. you don't *have* a daughter? Oh. Well, I guess I would like to speak to *you*, Mrs Wentworth . . .'

'Oh, Raunch, how *awful*!'

'Well, this is Dr Ronkers. I'm a urologist at University Hospital. Yes, *George* Ronkers. Dr George Ronkers. Well . . . hi. Yes, *George*. Oh, *Sarah*, is it? Well, Sarah . . .'

And with the end of the summer there came an end to the rearrangements of the Ronkers' interior space. Kit was through with carpentry and busy with her teaching and her school work. When the workmen left, and the tools were carried off, and the dismantled walls no longer lay heaped in the Ronkers' yard, it must have become apparent to Bardlong that reconstruction – at least for this year – was over.

The walnut tree was still there. Perhaps Bardlong had thought that in the course of the summer building, the tree would go – making way for a new wing. He couldn't have known that the Ronkers were rebuilding their house on the principle of 'inviting the tree in'.

With autumn coming on, Bardlong's issue with the black walnut tree grew clear. Old Herr Kesler had not been wrong. George and Kit had a premonition of it the first cool, windy night of the fall. They lay on the sleeping platform with the tree swirling around them and the yellowing leaves falling past them, and they heard what sounded like a candlepin bowling ball falling on their roof and thudding its way down the slope to score in the rain gutter.

'Raunch?'

'That was a goddamn *walnut*!' Ronkers said.

'It sounded like a brick out of the chimney,' Kit said.

And through the night they sat bolt upright to a few more: when the wind would loose one or a squirrel would successfully attack one, *whump!* it would strike, and roll *thunker-thunker-thunker-thunker dang!* into the clattering rain gutter.

'That one took a squirrel with it,' Ronkers said.

'Well,' said Kit, 'at least there's no mistaking it for a prowler. It's too obvious a noise.'

'Like a prowler dropping his instruments of burglary,' Ronkers said.

*Whump! thunker-thunker-thunker-thunker dang!*

'Like a prowler shot off the roof,' Kit groaned.

'We'll get used to it, I'm sure,' Ronkers said.

'Well, Raunch, I gather Bardlong has been slow to adapt . . .'

In the morning Ronkers noticed that the Bardlong house had a slate roof with a far steeper pitch than his own. He tried to imagine what the walnuts would sound like on Bardlong's roof.

'But there's surely an attic in that house,' Kit said. 'The sound is probably muffled.' Ronkers could not imagine the sound of a walnut striking a slate roof — and its subsequent descent to the rain gutter — as in any way 'muffled'.

By mid-October the walnuts were dropping with fearful regularity. Ronkers thought ahead to the first wild storm in November as a potential blitzkrieg. Kit went out to rake a pile of the fallen nuts together; she heard one cutting loose above her, ripping through the dense leaves. She thought against looking up — imagining the ugly bruise between her eyes and the blow of the back of her head driven into the ground. She bent over double and covered her head with her hands. The walnut narrowly missed her offered spine; it gave her a kidney punch. *Thok!*

'It *hurt,* Raunch,' she said.

A beaming Bardlong stood under the dangerous tree, watching Ronkers comfort his wife. Kit had not noticed him there before. He wore a thick Alpine hat with a ratty feather in it; it looked like a reject of Herr Kesler's.

'Kesler gave it to me,' Bardlong said. 'I had asked for a *helmet.'* He stood arrogantly in his yard, his rake held like a fungo bat, waiting for the tree to pitch a walnut down to him. He had chosen the perfect moment to introduce the subject — Kit just wounded, still in tears.

'You ever hear one of those things hit a slate roof?' Bardlong asked. 'I'll call you up the next time a whole clump's ready to drop. About three a.m.'

'It *is* a problem,' Ronkers agreed.

'But it's a *lovely* tree,' Kit said defensively.

'Well, it's *your* problem, of course,' Bardlong said, offhanded, cheerful. 'If I have the same problem with my rain gutters this fall as I had last, I *may* have to ask you to remove the part of your tree that's over *our* property, but you can do what you want with the rest of it.'

'*What* rain gutter problem?' Ronkers asked.

'It must happen to *your* rain gutters, too, I'm sure . . .'

'*What* happens?' asked Kit.

'They get full of goddamn walnuts,' Bardlong said. 'And it rains, and rains, and the gutters don't work because they're clogged with walnuts, and the water pours down the side of your house; your windows leak and your basement fills with water. That's all.'

'Oh.'

'Kesler bought me a mop. But he was a poor old foreigner, you know,' Bardlong said confidingly, 'and you never felt like getting *legal* with him. You know.'

'Oh,' said Kit. She did not like Bardlong. The casual cheerfulness of his tone seemed as removed from his meaning as the shock absorber trade was from those delicately laced trellises in his yard.

'Oh, I don't mind raking up a few nuts,' Bardlong said, smiling, 'or waking up a few times in the night, when I think storks are crash-landing on my roof.' He paused, glowing under old Kesler's hat. 'Or wearing the protective gear,' he added. He doffed the hat to Kit, who at the moment she saw his lightly freckled dome exposed was praying for that unmistakable sound of the leaves ripping apart above. But Bardlong returned the hat to his head. A walnut began its descent. Kit and George crouched, hands over their heads; Bardlong never flinched. With considerable force the walnut struck the slate-stone wall between them, splitting with a dramatic *kak!* It was as hard and as big as a baseball.

41

'It's sort of an *exciting* tree in the fall, really,' Bardlong said. 'Of course, my wife won't go near it this time of year – a sort of prisoner in her own yard, you might say.' He laughed; some gold fillings from the booming brake systems industry winked in his mouth. 'But that's all right. No price should be set for beauty, and it *is* a lovely tree. *Water damage,* though,' he said, and his tone changed suddenly, 'is *real* damage.'

Bardlong managed, Ronkers thought, to make 'real' sound like a legal term.

'And if you've got to spend the money to take down half the tree, you better face up to taking it all. When *your* basement's full of water, that won't be any joke.' Bardlong pronounced 'joke' as if it were an obscene word; moreover, the implication in Bardlong's voice led one to suspect the wisdom in thinking *anything* was funny.

Kit said, 'Well, Raunch, you could just get up on the roof and sweep the walnuts out of the rain gutters.'

'Of course *I'm* too old for that,' Bardlong sighed, as if getting up on his roof was something he *longed* to do.

'Raunch, you could even sweep out Mr Bardlong's rain gutters, couldn't you? Like once a week or so, just at this time of the year?'

Ronkers looked at the towering Bardlong roof, the smooth slate surface, the steep pitch. Headlines flooded his mind: DOCTOR TAKES FOUR STORY FALL! UROLOGIST BEANED BY NUT! CAREER CUT SHORT BY DEADLY TREE!

No, Ronkers understood the moment; it was time to look ahead to the larger victory; he could only win half. Bardlong was oblique, but Bardlong was clearly a man with a made-up mind.

'Could you recommend a tree surgeon?' Ronkers asked.

'Oh, *Raunch*!' said Kit.

'We'll cut the tree in half,' Ronkers said, striding boldly toward the split trunk, kicking the bomb-debris of fallen walnuts aside.

'I think about *here,*' Bardlong said eagerly, having no doubt picked the spot years ago. 'Of course, what *costs*,' he added, with the old shock absorber seriousness back in his voice, 'is properly roping the overhanging limbs so that they won't fall on my roof (*I hope they fall* through *your roof, Kit thought*). Whereas, if you cut the whole tree down,' Bardlong said, 'you could save some time, and your money, by just letting the whole thing fall along the line of the wall; there's room for it, you see, before the street . . .' The tree spread over them, obviously a *measured* tree, long in Bardlong's calculations. A terminal patient, Ronkers thought, perhaps from the beginning.

'I would like to keep the part of the tree that doesn't damage your property, Mr Bardlong,' Ronkers said; his dignity was good; his distance was cool. Bardlong respected the sense of business in his voice.

'I could arrange this for you,' Bardlong said. 'I mean, I know a good tree outfit.' Somehow, the 'outfit' smacked of the fleet of men driving around in the Bardlong trucks. 'It would cost you a little less,' he added, with his irritatingly confiding tone, 'if you let me set this up . . .'

Kit was about to speak but Ronkers said, 'I would really appreciate that, Mr Bardlong. And we'll just have to take our chances with *our* rain gutters.'

'Those are new windows,' Kit said. 'They won't leak. And who cares about water in the old basement? God, I don't care, I can tell you . . .'

Ronkers tried to return to Bardlong's patient and

infuriatingly *understanding* smile. It was a Yes-I-Tolerate-My-Wife-Too smile. Kit was hoping for a vast unloading from above in the walnut tree, a downfall which would leave them all as hurt as she felt they were guilty.

'Raunch,' she said later. 'What if poor old Mr Kesler sees it? And he *will* see it, Raunch. He comes by, from time to time, you know. What are you going to tell him about selling out his tree?'

'I didn't sell it out!' Ronkers said. 'I think I saved what I could of the tree by letting him have his half. I couldn't have stopped him, legally. You must have seen that.'

'What about poor Mr Kesler, though?' Kit said. 'We *promised*.'

'Well, the tree will still be here.'

'Half the tree . . .'

'Better than none.'

'But what will he think of us?' Kit asked. 'He'll think we agree with Bardlong that the tree is a nuisance. He'll think it will only be a matter of time before we cut down the rest.'

'Well, the tree *is* a nuisance, Kit.'

'I just want to know what you're going to say to Mr Kesler, Raunch.'

'I won't have to say anything,' Ronkers told her. 'Kesler's in the hospital.'

She seemed stunned to hear that, old Kesler always having struck her with a kind of peasant heartiness. Those men must live forever, surely? 'Raunch?' she asked, less sure of herself now. 'He'll get out of the hospital, won't he? And what will you tell him when he gets out and comes around to see his tree?'

'He won't get out,' Ronkers told her.

'Oh *no,* Raunch . . .'

The phone rang. He usually let Kit answer the phone; she could fend off the calls that weren't serious. But Kit was deep in a vision of old Kesler, in his worn lederhosen with his skinny, hairless legs.

'Hello,' Ronkers told the phone.

'Dr Ronkers?'

'Yes,' he said.

'This is Margaret Brant.' Ronkers groped to place the name. A young girl's voice?

'Uh . . .'

'You left a message at the dorm to have me call this number,' Margaret Brant said. And Ronkers remembered, then; he looked over the list of the women he had to call this week. Their names were opposite the names of their infected partners-in-fun.

'Miss Brant?' he said. Kit was mouthing words like a mute: *Why* won't old Mr Kesler ever get out of the hospital? 'Miss Brant, do you know a young man named Harlan Booth?'

Miss Brant seemed mute herself now, and Kit whispered harshly, *'What?* What's wrong with him?'

'Cancer,' he whispered back.

'Yes. *What?'* said Margaret Brant. 'Yes, I know Harlan Booth. What is the matter, please?'

'I am treating Harlan Booth for gonorrhea, Miss Brant,' Ronkers said. There was no reaction over the phone. 'Clap?' Ronkers said. 'Gonorrhea? Harlan Booth has the clap.'

'I know what you mean,' the girl said. Her voice had gone hard; she was suspicious. Kit was turned away from him so that he couldn't see her face.

'If you have a gynecologist here in town, Miss Brant, I think you should make an appointment. I

45

could recommend Dr Caroline Gilmore; her office is at University Hospital. Or, of course, you could come to see me . . .'

'Look, who *is* this?' Margaret Brant said. 'How do I know you're a doctor? Someone just left a phone number for me to call. I never had anything to do with Harlan Booth. What kind of dirty joke is this?'

Possible, thought Ronkers. Harlan Booth had been a vain, uncooperative kid who had very scornfully feigned casualness when asked who else might be infected. 'Could be a lot of people,' he'd said proudly. And Ronkers had been forced to press him to get even one name: Margaret Brant. Possibly a virgin whom Harlan Booth disliked?

'You can call me at my home phone after I hang up,' Ronkers said. 'It's listed in the book: Dr George Ronkers . . . and see if it's not the same number you have now. Or else I can simply apologize for the mistake; I can call up Harlan Booth and tell him off. And,' Ronkers gambled, 'you can examine yourself for any discharge, especially in the morning, and see if there's any inflammation. And if you think there's a possibility, you can certainly see another doctor and I'll never know. But if you've had relations with Harlan Booth, Miss Brant, I . . .'

She hung up.

'Cancer?' Kit said, her back still to him. 'Cancer of what?'

'Lungs,' Ronkers said. 'The bronchoscopy was positive; they didn't even have to open him up.'

The phone rang again. When Ronkers said hello, the party hung up. Ronkers had a deplorable habit of visualizing people he had only spoken with on the phone. He saw Margaret Brant in the girls' dormitory. First she would turn to the dictionary. Then, moving

46

lights and mirrors, she would *look* at herself. What *should* it look like? she would be wondering. And perhaps a trip to the rack of medical encyclopedias in the library. Or, last, a talk with a friend. An embarrassing phone call to Harlan Booth? No, Ronkers couldn't see that part.

He could see Kit examining her walnut-bruise in the multi-imaged mirror which was suspended beside the inverted cone – also suspended – which was the flue for the open-pit fireplace in their bedroom. One day, Ronkers thought, I will fall off the sleeping platform into the open-pit fireplace and run screaming and burning through the bedroom seeing myself times five in that multi-imaged mirror. Jesus.

'One walnut sure makes a lot of bruises,' Ronkers said sleepily.

'Please don't touch it,' Kit said. She had wanted to bring up another subject tonight, but her enthusiasm had been stolen.

Outside, the doomed tree – the would-be amputee – brushed against their window the way a cat brushes against your leg. In that high room, the way the wind nudged under the eaves made sleep feel precarious – as if the roof might be suddenly lifted off the house and they'd be left there, exposed. The final phase of achieving perfect interior space.

Sometime after midnight, Ronkers was called to the hospital for an emergency. An old woman, whose entire urinary system Ronkers had replaced with bags and hoses, was suffering perhaps her last malfunction. Five minutes after he left the house, Kit answered the phone. It was the hospital saying that the woman had died and there was no need to hurry.

George was gone two hours; Kit lay awake. She had

so much she wanted to say when George got back that she was overwhelmed with where to begin; she let him fall asleep. She had wanted to discuss once more whether and when they would have children. But the night seemed so stalked by mayhem that the optimism of having babies struck her as absurd. She thought instead of the cool aesthetics, the thin economy, which characterized her leanings in the field of architecture.

She lay awake a long time after George fell asleep, listening to the restless rubbing of the tree, hearing the patternless, breakaway falls of the walnuts hurtling down on them – dropping into their lives as randomly as old Herr Kesler's cancer, as Margaret Brant's possible case of clap.

In Ronkers' office, waiting for him even before his receptionist had arrived, was a bird-boned girl with a yogurt-and-wheat-germ complexion who couldn't have been more than eighteen; her clothes were expensive-looking and conservative – a steel-toned suit her mother might have worn. A cream-coloured, softly scented scarf was at her throat. Ronkers thought she was beautiful; she looked as if she'd just stepped off a yacht. But, of course, he knew who she was.

'Margaret Brant?' he asked, shaking her hand. Her eyes were a complement to her suit, an eerie dawn-gray. She had a perfect nose, wide nostrils in which, Ronkers thought, hair would not dare to grow.

'Dr Ronkers?'

'Yes. Margaret Brant?'

'Of course,' she sighed. She eyed the stirrups on Ronkers' examining table with a bitter dread.

'I'm awfully sorry, Miss Brant, to have called you, but Harlan Booth was not the most co-operative patient

48

I've ever had, and I thought – for your own good – since *he* wouldn't call you, I should.' The girl nodded, biting her lower lip. She absently removed her suit jacket and her English buckle shoes; she moved toward the examining table and those gleaming stirrups as if the whole contraption were a horse she was not sure how to mount.

'You want to *look* at me?' she asked, her back to Ronkers.

'Please relax,' Ronkers begged her. 'This isn't especially unpleasant, really. Have you had any discharge? Have you noticed any burning, any inflammation?'

'I haven't noticed *anything*,' the girl told him, and Ronkers saw she was about to burst into tears. 'It's very unfair!' she cried suddenly. 'I've always been so careful with . . . sex,' she said, 'and I really didn't allow very much of *anything,* with Harlan Booth. I *hate* Harlan Booth!' she screamed. 'I didn't know he had anything wrong with him, of course, or I never would have let him *touch* me!'

'But you *did* let him?' Ronkers asked. He was confused.

' . . . *touch* me?' she said. 'Yes, he touched me . . . *there*, you know. And he kissed me, a *lot*. But I wouldn't let him do anything *else*!' she cried. 'And he was just *awful* about it, too, and he probably knew then that he was giving me *this*!'

'You mean, he just *kissed* you?' Ronkers asked, incredulous.

'Well, *yes*. And *touched* me, you know,' she said, blushing. 'He put his hand in my pants!' she cried. 'And I *let* him!' She collapsed against the bent-knee part of one stirrup on the examining table and Ronkers went over to her and led her very gently to a chair beside his desk. She sobbed, with her little sharp-boned fists balled against her eyes.

'Miss Brant,' Ronkers said. 'Miss Brant, do you mean that Harlan Booth only touched you with his *hand*? You didn't have *real* sexual intercourse . . . Miss Brant?'

She looked up at him, shocked. 'God, *no!*' she said. She bit the back of her hand and kept her fierce eyes on Ronkers.

'Just his *hand* touched you . . . *there*?' said Ronkers, and he brushed the lap of her suit skirt when he said 'there'.

'Yes,' she said.

Ronkers took her small face in his hands and smiled at her. He was not very good at comforting or reassuring people. People seemed to misread his gestures. Margaret Brant seemed to think he was going to kiss her passionately on the mouth, because her eyes grew very wide and her back stiffened and her quick hands came up under his wrists, trying to shove him away.

'Margaret!' Ronkers said. 'You *can't* have the clap if that's all that happened. You don't often catch a venereal disease from someone's *hand*.'

She now held his wrists as though they were important to her. 'But he *kissed* me, too,' she said worriedly. 'With his *mouth*,' she added, to make things clear.

Ronkers shook his head. He went to his desk and gathered up a bunch of medical pamphlets on venereal disease. The pamphlets resembled brochures from travel agencies; there were lots of pictures of people smiling sympathetically.

'Harlan Booth must have wanted me to embarrass you,' Ronkers said. 'I think he was angry that you wouldn't let him . . . *you* know.'

'Then you don't even have to *look* at me?' she asked.

'No,' Ronkers said. 'I'm sure I don't.'

'I've never *been* looked at, you know,' Margaret Brant told him. Ronkers didn't know what to say. 'I mean, *should* I be looked at? – somet:me, you know. Just to see if everything's all right?'

'Well, you might have a standard examination by a gynecologist. I can recommend Dr Caroline Gilmore at University Hospital; a lot of students find her very nice.'

'But *you* don't want to look at me?' she asked.

'Uh, no,' Ronkers said. 'There's no need. And for a standard examination, you should see a gynecologist. I'm a urologist.'

'Oh.'

She looked vacantly at the examining table and those waiting stirrups; she slipped into her suit jacket very gracefully; she had a bit more hardship with her shoes.

'Boy, that Harlan Booth is going to *get* it,' she said suddenly, and with a surprising authority in her small, sharp voice.

'Harlan Booth has already *got* it,' Ronkers said, trying to lighten the situation. But tiny Margaret Brant looked newly dangerous to him. 'Please don't do anything you'll regret,' Ronkers began weakly. But the girl's clean, wide nostrils were flaring, her gun-gray eyes were dancing.

'Thank you, Dr Ronkers,' Margaret Brant said with icy poise. 'I very much appreciate your taking the trouble, and putting up with the embarrassment, of calling me.' She shook his hand. 'You are a very brave and *moral* man,' she said, as if she were conferring military honors on Ronkers.

Watch out, Harlan Booth, he thought. Margaret Brant

left Ronkers' office like a woman who had strapped on those stirrups for a ride on the examining table – and won.

Ronkers phoned up Harlan Booth. He certainly wasn't thinking of warning him; he wanted some right names. Harlan Booth took so long to answer the phone that Ronkers had worked himself up pretty well by the time Booth said a sleepy 'Hello'.

'You lying bastard, Booth,' Ronkers said. 'I want the names of people you've actually slept with – people who actually might have been exposed to your case, or from whom you might even have *gotten* it.'

'Oh go to hell, Doc,' Booth said, bored. 'How'd you like little Maggie Brant?'

'That was dirty,' Ronkers said. 'A rather young and innocent girl, Booth. You were very mean.'

'A little prig, a stuck-up rich bitch,' Harlan Booth said. 'Did you have any luck with her, Doc?'

'Please,' Ronkers said. 'Just give me some names. Be kind, you've got to be kind, Booth.'

'Queen Elizabeth,' Booth said. 'Tuesday Weld, Pearl Buck . . .'

'Bad taste, Booth,' Ronkers said. 'Don't be a swine.'

'Bella Abzug,' Booth said. 'Gloria Steinem, Raquel Welch, Mamie Eisenhower . . .'

Ronkers hung up. *Go get him if you can, Maggie Brant; I wish you luck!*

There was a crush of people in the waiting room outside his office; Ronkers peered out the letter slot at them. His receptionist caught the secret signal and flashed his phone light.

'Yes?'

'You're supposed to call your wife. You want me to hold up the throng a minute?'

'Thank you, yes.'

Kit must have picked up the phone and immediately shoved the mouthpiece toward the open window, because Ronkers heard the unmistakably harsh *yowl* of a chain saw (maybe, *two* chain saws).

'Well,' Kit said, 'this is some tree outfit, all right. Didn't Bardlong say he'd fix it up with a good *tree* outfit?'

'Yes,' Ronkers said. 'What's wrong?'

'Well, there are three men here with chain saws and helmets with their names printed on them. Their names are Mike, Joe, and Dougie. Dougie is the highest up in the tree right now; I hope he breaks his thick neck . . .'

'Kit, for God's sake, what's the matter?'

'Oh, Raunch, they're not a *tree* outfit at all. They're Bardlong's men – you know, they came in a goddamn BARDLONG STOPS YOU SHORT truck.

'They'll probably kill the whole tree,' Kit said. 'You can't just hack off limbs and branches without putting that *stuff* on, can you?'

'Stuff?'

'Goop? Gunk?' Kit said. 'You know, that gooey black stuff. It *heals* the tree. God, Raunch, you're supposed to be a *doctor*, I thought you'd know something about it.'

'I'm not a *tree* doctor,' Ronkers said.

'These men don't even look like they know what they're doing,' Kit said. 'They've got ropes all over the tree and they're swinging back and forth on the ropes, and every once in a while they buzz something off with those damn saws.'

'I'll call Bardlong,' Ronkers said.

But his phone light was flashing. He saw three patients in rapid order, gained four minutes on his appointment schedule, peeked through the letter slot, pleaded with his receptionist, took three minutes off to call Bardlong.

'I thought you were hiring *professionals*,' Ronkers said.

'These men are *very* professional,' Bardlong told him.

'Professional *shock absorber* men,' Ronkers said.

'No, no,' Bardlong said. 'Dougie used to be a tree man.'

'Specialized in the walnut tree, too, I'll bet.'

'Everything's fine,' Bardlong said.

'I see why it costs me less,' Ronkers said. 'I end up paying *you*.'

'I'm retired,' Bardlong said.

Ronkers' phone light was flashing again; he was about to hang up.

'Please don't worry,' Bardlong said. 'Everything is in good hands.' And then there was an ear-splitting disturbance that made Ronkers sweep his desk ashtray into the wastebasket. From Bardlong's end of the phone came a rending sound – glassy, Baroque chandeliers falling to a ballroom floor? Mrs Bardlong, or some equally shrill and elderly woman, hooted and howled.

'Good *Christ*!' Bardlong said over the phone. And to Ronkers he hastily added, 'Excuse me.' He hung up, but Ronkers had distinctly heard it: a splintering of wood, a shattering of glass, and the yammer of a chain saw 'invited in' the house. He tried to imagine the tree man, Dougie, falling with a roped limb through the Bardlongs' bay window, his chain saw still sawing as he snarled his way through the velvet drapes and the chaise longue. Mrs Bardlong, an ancient cat on her lap, would have been reading the paper, when . . .

But his receptionist was flashing him with mad regularity, and Ronkers gave in. He saw a four-year-old girl with a urinary infection (little girls are more susceptible to that than little boys); he saw a forty-eight-year-old man with a large and exquisitely tender prostate; he saw a twenty-five-year-old woman who was suffering her first bladder problem. He prescribed some Azo Gantrisin for her; he found a sample packet of the big red choke-a-horse pills and gave it to her. She stared at them, frightened at the size.

'Is there, you know, an *applicator*?' she asked.

'No, no,' Ronkers said. 'You take them *orally*. You swallow them.'

The phone flashed. Ronkers knew it was Kit.

'What happened?' he asked her. 'I *heard* it!'

'Dougie cut right through the limb *and* the rope that was guiding the limb away from the house,' Kit said.

'How exciting!'

'Poked the limb through Bardlong's bathroom window like a great pool cue . . .'

'Oh,' said Ronkers, disappointed. He had hoped for the bay . . .

'I think Mrs Bardlong was in the bathroom,' Kit said.

Shocked at his glee, Ronkers asked, 'Was anyone hurt?'

'Dougie sawed into Mike's arm,' Kit said, 'and I think Joe broke his ankle jumping out of the tree.'

'God!'

'No one's badly hurt,' Kit said. 'But the tree looks *awful*; they didn't even finish it.'

'Bardlong will have to take care of it,' Ronkers said.

'Raunch,' Kit said. 'The newspaper photographer was here; he goes out on every ambulance call. He took a picture of the tree and Bardlong's window. Listen, this is *serious*, Raunch: Does Kesler get a newspaper on his breakfast tray? You've got to speak to the floor nurse; don't let him see the picture, Raunch. Okay?'

'Okay,' he said.

Outside in the waiting room the woman was showing the Azo Gantrisin pills to Ronkers' receptionist. 'He wants me to *swallow* them . . .' Ronkers let the letter slot close slowly. He buzzed his receptionist.

'Entertain them, please,' he said. 'I am taking ten.'

He slipped out of his office through the hospital entrance and crossed through Emergency as the ambulance staff was bringing in a man on a stretcher; he was propped up on his elbows, his ankle unbooted and wrapped in an ice pack. His helmet said 'Joe'. The man who walked beside the stretcher carried his helmet in his one good hand. He was 'Mike'. His other hand was held up close to his breast; his forearm was blood-soaked; an ambulance attendant walked alongside with his thumb jammed deep into the crook of Mike's arm. Ronkers intercepted them and took a look at the cut. It was not serious, but it was a messy, ragged thing with a lot of black oil and sawdust in it. About thirty stitches, Ronkers guessed, but the man was not bleeding too badly. A tedious debridement, lots of Xylocaine . . . but Fowler was covering Emergency this morning, and it wasn't any of Ronkers' business.

He went on to the third floor. Kesler was in 339, a single room; at least a private death awaited him. Ronkers found the floor nurse, but Kesler's door was open and Ronkers stood with the nurse in the hall where the old man could see them; Kesler recognized Ronkers, but didn't seem to know *where* he recognized Ronkers from.

'*Kommen Sie hinein, bitte!*' Kesler called. His voice

56

was like speech scraped on a file, sanded down to something scratchier than old records. *'Grüss Gott!'* he called.

'I wish I knew some German,' the nurse told Ronkers.

Ronkers knew a little. He went into Kesler's room, made a cursory check on the movable parts now keeping him alive. The rasp in Kesler's voice was due to the Levine tube which ran down his throat to his stomach.

'Hello, Mr Kesler,' Ronkers said. 'Do you remember me?' Kesler stared with wonder at Ronkers; they had taken out his false teeth and his face was curiously turtlelike in its leatheriness – its sagging, cold qualities. Predictably, he had lost about sixty pounds.

*'Ach!'* Kesler said suddenly. 'Das house gebought? You . . . *ja!* How goes it? Your wife the walls downtook?'

'Yes,' Ronkers said, 'but you would like it. It's very beautiful. There's more window light now.'

*'Und der Bardlong?'* Kesler whispered. 'He has not the tree down-chopped?'

'No.'

*'Sehr gut!'* Herr Kesler said. That is pronounced *zehr goot.* 'Gut boy!' Kesler told Ronkers. *Goot buoy.* Kesler blinked his dull, dry eyes for a second and when they opened it was as if they opened on another scene – another time, somewhere. *'Frühstück?'* he asked politely.

'That means breakfast,' Ronkers told the nurse. They had Kesler on a hundred milligrams of Demerol every four hours; that makes you less than alert.

Ronkers was getting out of the elevator on the first floor when the intercom paged 'Dr Heart'. There was no Dr Heart at University Hospital. 'Dr Heart' meant that someone's heart had stopped.

'Dr Heart?' the intercom asked sweetly. 'Please come to 304 . . .'

Any doctor in the hospital was supposed to hurry to that room. There was an unwritten rule that you looked around and made a slow move to the nearest elevator, hoping another doctor would beat you to the patient. Ronkers hesitated, letting the elevator door close. He pushed the button again, but the elevator was already moving up.

'Dr Heart, room 304,' the intercom said calmly. It was better than urgently crying, 'A doctor! Any doctor to room 304! Oh my God, *hurry*!' That might disturb the other patients and the visitors.

Dr Hampton was coming down the floor toward the elevator.

'You still having office calls?' Hampton asked Ronkers.

'Yup,' Ronkers said.

'Go back to your office, then,' Hampton said. 'I'll get this one.'

The elevator had stopped on the third floor; it was pretty certain that 'Dr Heart' had already arrived in 304. Ronkers went back to his office. It would be nice to take Kit out to dinner, he thought.

At the Route Six Ming Dynasty, Kit ordered the sweet and sour bass; Ronkers chose the beef in lobster sauce. He was distracted. He had seen a sign in the window of the Route Six M.ng Dynasty, just as they'd come in the door. It was a sign about two feet long and one foot high – black lettering on white shirt cardboard, perhaps. It looked perfectly natural there in the window, for it was about the expected size – and, Ronkers falsely assumed, about the expected content of a sign like TWO WAITRESSES WANTED.

Ronkers was distracted only now, as he sipped a drink with Kit, because only now was the *real* content of that sign coming through to him. He thought he was imagining it, so he excused himself from the table and slipped outside the Route Six Ming Dynasty to have another look at that sign.

Appallingly, he had *not* imagined it. There, vividly in a lower corner of the window, plainly in view of every customer approaching the door, was a neatly lettered sign which read: HARLAN BOOTH HAS THE CLAP.

'Well, it's *true,* isn't it?' Kit asked.

'Well, yes, but that's not the point,' Ronkers said. 'It's sort of unethical. I mean, it *has* to be Margaret Brant, and I'm responsible for releasing the information. That sort of thing should be confidential, after all . . .'

'Turds,' said Kit. 'Good for Margaret Brant! You must admit, Raunch, if Harlan Booth had played fair with you, the whole thing wouldn't have happened. I think he deserves it.'

'Well, of course he *deserves* it,' Ronkers said, 'but I wonder where *else* she put up signs.'

'Really, Raunch, just let it be . . .'

But Ronkers had to see for himself. They drove to the Student Union. Inside the main lobby, Ronkers searched the giant bulletin board for clues.

'70 BMW, LIKE NEW . . .

RIDERS WANTED TO SHARE EXPENSES AND DRIVING TO NYC, LV. THURS., RETURN MON. EVE, CALL 'LARRY', 351-4306 . . .

HARLAN BOOTH HAS THE CLAP . . .

'My God.'

They went to the auditorium; a play was in progress. They didn't even have to get out of their car to see it: a NO PARKING sign had been neatly covered and given the new message. Kit was hysterical.

The Whale Room was where a lot of students drank and played pool and danced to local talent. It was a loud, smoke-filled place; Ronkers had several emergency calls a month involving patients who had begun their emergency in the Whale Room.

Somehow, Margaret Brant had warmed the bartender's heart. Above the bar mirror, above the glowing bottles, above the sign saying CHECKS CASHED FOR EXACT AMOUNT ONLY, were the same neat and condemning letters now familiar to Ronkers and Kit. The Whale Room was informed that Harlan Booth was contagious.

Fearing the worst, Ronkers insisted they take a drive past Margaret Brant's dorm – a giant building, a women's dormitory of prison size and structure. Ivy did not grow there.

In the upcast streetlights, above the bicycle racks – seemingly tacked to every sill of every third-floor window – a vast sewn-together bed-sheet stretched across the entire front of Catherine Cascomb Dormitory for Women. Margaret Brant had friends. Her friends were upset, too. In a massive sacrifice of linen and labor, every girl in every third-floor, front-window room had done her part. Each letter was about six feet high and single-bed width.

'Fantastic!' Kit shouted. 'Well done! Good show! Let him have it!'

'Way to go, Maggie Brant,' whispered Ronkers reverently. But he knew he hadn't seen the end of it.

It was two a.m. when the phone rang and he suspected it was not the hospital.

'Yes?' he said.

'Did I wake you up, Doc?' said Harlan Booth. 'I sure *hope* I woke you up.'

'Hello, Booth,' Ronkers said. Kit sat up beside him, looking strong and fit.

'Call off your goons, Doc. I don't have to put up with this. This is harassment. You're supposed to be *ethical*, you crummy doctors . . .'

'You mean you've seen the signs?' Ronkers asked.

*'Signs?'* Booth asked. *'What* signs? What are you talking about?'

'What are *you* talking about?' Ronkers said, genuinely puzzled.

'You know goddamn well what I'm talking about!' Harlan Booth yelled. 'Every half-hour a broad calls me up. It's two o'clock in the morning, Doc, and every half-hour a broad calls me up. *A different* broad, every half-hour, you know perfectly well . . .'

'What do they say to you?' Ronkers asked.

'Cut it out!' Booth yelled. 'You know damn well what they say to me, Doc. They say stuff like, "How's your clap coming along, Mr Booth?" and "Where are you spreading your clap around, Harlan old baby?" You *know* what they say to me, Doc!'

'Cheer up, Booth,' Ronkers said. 'Get out for a breath of air. Take a drive – down by Catherine Cascomb Dormitory for Women, for example. There's a lovely banner unfurled in your honor; you really ought to see it.'

'A *banner*?' Booth said.

'Go get a drink at the Whale Room, Booth,' Ronkers told him. 'It will settle you down.'

*'Look,* Doc!' Booth screamed. 'You call them off!'

'I didn't call them on, Booth.'

'It's that little bitch Maggie Brant, isn't it, Doc?'

'I doubt she's operating alone, Booth.'

'Look,' Booth said. 'I can take you to court for this. Invasion of privacy. I can go to the papers. I'll go to the *university* – expose Student Health. You've got no right to be this unethical.'

'Why not just call Margaret Brant?' Ronkers suggested.

'*Call* her?'

'And apologize,' Ronkers said. 'Tell her you're sorry.'

'*Sorry?!*' Booth shouted.

'And then come give me some names,' Ronkers said.

'I'm going to every newspaper in the state, Doc.'

'I'd love to see you do that, Booth. They would crucify you . . .'

'Doc . . .'

'Give yourself a real lift, Booth. Take a drive by Catherine Cascomb Dormitory for Women . . .'

'Go to hell, Doc.'

'Better hurry, Booth. Tomorrow they may start the bumper sticker campaign.'

'Bumper stickers?'

'"Harlan Booth has the clap",' Ronkers said. 'That's what the bumper stickers are going to say . . .'

Booth hung up. The way he hung up rang in Ronkers' ear for a long time. The walnuts dropping on the roof were almost soothing after the sound Booth had made.

'I think we've got him,' Ronkers told Kit.

'"*We,*" is it?' she said. 'You sound like you've joined up.'

'I have,' Ronkers said. 'I'm going to call Margaret

62

Brant first thing in the morning and tell her about my bumper sticker idea.'

But Margaret Brant needed no coaching. In the morning when Ronkers went out to his car, there was a freshly stuck-on bumper sticker, front and back. Dark blue lettering on a bright yellow background; it ran half the length of the bumper.

### HARLAN BOOTH HAS THE CLAP

On his way to the hospital, Ronkers saw more of the adorned cars. Some drivers were parked in gas stations, working furiously to remove the stickers. But that was a hard, messy job. Most people appeared to be too busy to do anything about the stickers right away.

'I counted thirty-four, just driving across town,' Ronkers told Kit on the phone. 'And it's still early in the morning.'

'Bardlong got to work early, too,' Kit told him.

'What do you mean?'

'He hired a real *tree* outfit this time. The tree surgeons came right after you left.'

'Ah, real tree surgeons . . .'

'They have helmets, too, and their names are Mickey, Max, and Harv,' Kit said. 'And they brought a whole tub of that black healing stuff.'

'*Dr Heart,*' said Ronkers' receptionist, cutting in. '*Dr Heart, please, to 339.*'

'Raunch?'

But the receptionist was interrupting because it was so early; there just might not be another doctor around the hospital. Ronkers came in early, often hours ahead of his first appointment – to make his hospital rounds, yes, but mainly to sit in his office alone for a while.

'I've got to go,' he told Kit. 'I'll call back.'

'Who's Dr Hart?' Kit asked. 'Somebody new?'

'Yup,' Ronkers said, but he was thinking: No, it's probably somebody *old*.

He was out of his office, and half through the connecting tunnel which links the main hospital to several doctors' offices, when he heard the intercom call for Dr Heart again and recognized the room number: 339. That was old Herr Kesler's room, Ronkers remembered. Nurses, seeing him coming, opened doors for him; they opened doors in all directions, down all corridors, and they always looked after him a little disappointed that he did not pass through *their* doors, that he veered left instead of right. When he got to Kesler's room, the cardiac resuscitation cart was parked beside the bed and Dr Heart was already there. It was Danfors – a better Dr Heart than Ronkers could have been, Ronkers knew; Danfors was a heart specialist.

Kesler was dead. That is, technically, when your heart stops, you're dead. But Danfors was already holding the electrode plates alongside Kesler's chest; the old man was about to get a tremendous jolt. Ah, the new machines, Ronkers marveled. Ronkers had once brought a man from the dead with five hundred volts from the cardioverter, lifting the body right off the bed, the limbs jangling – like pithing a frog in Introductory Biology.

'How's Kit, George?' Danfors asked.

'Just fine,' Ronkers said. Danfors was checking the i.v. of sodium bicarbonate running into Kesler. 'You must come see what she's done to the house. And bring Lilly.'

'Right-O,' said Danfors, giving Kesler five hundred volts.

Kesler's jaw was rigid on his chest and his teeth were clenched together fast, yet he managed to force a ghastly quarter-moon of a smile and expel a sentence of considerable volume and energy. It was German, of course, which surprised Danfors; he probably didn't know Kesler was an Austrian.

*'Noch ein Bier!'* Kesler ordered.

'What'd he say?' Danfors asked Ronkers.

'One more beer,' Ronkers translated.

But the current, of course, was cut. Kesler was dead again. Five hundred volts had woken him up, but Kesler did not have enough voltage of his own to keep himself awake.

'Shit,' Danfors said. 'I got three in a row with this thing when the hospital first got it, and I thought it was the best damn machine alive. But then I lost four out of the next five. So I was four-and-four with the thing; nothing is foolproof, of course. And now this one's the tie breaker.' Danfors managed to make his record with the heart machine sound like a losing season.

Now Ronkers didn't want to call Kit back; he knew Kesler's death would upset her. But she called him before he could work it out.

'Well, good,' Ronkers said.

'Raunch?' Kit asked. 'Kesler didn't see the paper, did he? They put the picture right on the front page, you know. You don't think he saw it, do you?'

'For a fact, he did not see it,' Ronkers said.

'Oh, good,' she said. She seemed to want to stay on the phone, Ronkers thought, although she wasn't talking. He told her he was awfully busy and he had to go.

Ronkers was in a mean mood when he sat down to lunch with Danfors in the hospital cafeteria. They were still on the soup course when the intercom pleasantly asked for Dr Heart. Since he was a heart specialist, Danfors answered most of the Dr Heart calls in the hospital whenever he was there, even if someone beat him to the elevator. He stood up and drank his milk down with a few swift guzzles.

*'Noch ein Bier!'* Ronkers said.

At home, Kit – the receiver of messages, the composer of rooms – had news for him. First, Margaret Brant had left word she was dropping the Harlan Booth assault because Booth had called and begged her forgiveness. Second, Booth had called and left Kit with a list of names. 'Real ones,' he'd said. Third, something was up with Bardlong and the infernal tree. The tree surgeons had alarmed him about something, and Bardlong and his wife had been poking about under the tree, along their side of the slate-stone wall, as if inspecting some new damage – as if plotting some new attack.

Wearily, Ronkers wandered to the yard to confront this new problem. Bardlong was down on the ground on all fours, peering deep into the caves of his slate-stone wall. Looking for squirrels?

'After the men did such a neat job,' Bardlong announced, 'it came to their attention that they should really have taken the whole thing down. And they're professionals, of course. I'm afraid they're right. The whole thing's got to come down.'

'Why?' Ronkers asked. He was trying to summon resistance but he found his resistance was stale.

'The roots,' Bardlong said. 'The roots are going to topple the wall. The *roots*,' he said again, as if he were

66

saying, *the armies! the tanks! the big guns!* 'The roots are crawling their way through my wall.' He made it sound like a conspiracy, the roots engaged in strangling some stones, bribing others. They crept their way into revolutionary positions among the slate. On signal, they were ready to upheave the whole.

'That will surely take some time,' Ronkers said, thinking, with a harshness that surprised him: That wall will outlive *you*, Bardlong!

'It's already happening,' Bardlong said. 'I hate to ask you to do this, of course, but the wall, if it crumbles, well . . .'

'We can build it up again,' Ronkers said. Ah, the *doctor* in him!

As illogical as cancer, Bardlong shook his head. Not far away, Ronkers saw, would be the line about hoping not to get 'legal'. Ronkers felt too tired to resist *anything*.

'It's simple,' said Bardlong. 'I want to keep the wall, you want to keep the tree.'

'Walls can be rebuilt,' Ronkers said, utterly without conviction.

'I see,' Bardlong said. Meaning what? It was like the five hundred volts administered to Kesler. There was a real effect – it was visible – but it was not effective at all. On his gloomy way back inside his house Ronkers pondered the effect of five hundred volts on Bardlong. With the current on for about five minutes.

He also fantasized this bizarre scene: Bardlong suddenly in Ronkers' office, looking at the floor and saying, 'I have had certain . . . relations, ah, with a lady who, ah, apparently was not in the best of . . . health.'

'If it would, Mr Bardlong, spare you any embarrassment,' Ronkers imagined himself saying, 'I could of course let the, ah, lady know that she should seek medical attention.'

'You'd do that for me?' Bardlong would cry then, overcome. 'Why, I mean, I would, ah . . . pay you for that, anything you ask.'

And Ronkers would have him then, of course. With a hunting cat's leer, he would spring the price. 'How about half a walnut tree?'

But things like that, Ronkers knew, didn't happen. Things like that were in the nature of the stories about abandoned pets, limping their way from Vermont to California, finding the family months later, arriving with bleeding pads and wagging tails. The reason such stories were so popular was that they went pleasantly against what everyone knew *really* happened. The pet was squashed by a Buick in Massachusetts – or, worse, was perfectly happy to remain abandoned in Vermont.

And if Bardlong came to Ronkers' office, it would be for some perfectly respectable aspect of age finally lodging in his prostate.

'Kesler's dead, Kit,' Ronkers told her. 'His heart stopped, saved him a lot of trouble, really; he would have gotten quite uncomfortable.'

He held her in the fabulous sleeping place she had invented. Outside their window the scrawny, pruned tree clicked against the rain gutter like light bones. The leaves were all gone; what few walnuts remained were small and shriveled – even the squirrels ignored them, and if one had fallen on the roof it would have gone unnoticed. Winter-bare and offering nothing but its weird shadows on their bed and its alarming sounds throughout their night, the tree seemed hardly worth their struggle. Kesler, after all, was dead. And

Bardlong was so *very* retired that he had more time and energy to give to trivia than anyone who was likely to oppose him. The wall between Ronkers and Bardlong seemed frail, indeed.

It was then that Ronkers realized he had not made love to his wife in a very long time, and he made the sort of love to Kit that some therapist might have called 're-assuring'. And some lover, Ronkers thought later, might have called dull.

He watched her sleep. A lovely woman; her students, he suspected, cared for more than her architecture. And she, one day, might care more for them – or for *one* of them. Why was he thinking *that*? he wondered, then pondered his own recent sensations for the X-ray technician.

But those kinds of problems, for Kit and him, seemed years away – well, *months* away, at least.

He thought of Margaret Brant's sweet taste of revenge; her mature forgiveness surprised and encouraged him. And Harlan Booth's giving in? Whether he was converted – or just trapped, and evil to the core – was quite unknowable at the moment. Whether *anyone* was . . . Ronkers wondered.

Danfors' season with the heart machine now stood at four-and-six. What sort of odds were those in favor of human reproduction? – Ronkers' and Kit's, especially . . . And even if all the high school principals and parents in the world were as liberal and humorous and completely approachable concerning venereal disease, as they might be sympathetic toward a football injury, there would *still* be rampant clap in the world – and syphilis, and more.

Kit slept.

The brittle tree clacked against the house like the bill

69

of a parrot he remembered hearing in a zoo. Where was that? *What zoo?*

In an impulse, which felt to Ronkers like resignation, he moved to the window and looked over the moonlit roofs of the suburbs – many of which he could see for the first time, now that the leaves were all gone and a winter view was possible. And to all the people under those roofs, and more, he whispered, wickedly, 'Have fun!' To Ronkers, this was a kind of benediction with a hidden hook.

'Why *not* have children?' he said aloud. Kit stirred, but she had not actually heard him.

# ALMOST IN IOWA

The driver relied on travel as a form of reflection, but the Volvo had never been out of Vermont. The driver was an officious traveler; he kept his oil up and his windshield clean and he carried his own tire gauge in his left breast pocket next to a ball-point pen. The pen was for making entries in the Grand Trip List, such things as gas mileage, toll fees and riding time.

The Volvo appreciated this carefulness of the driver; Route 9 across Vermont, Brattleboro to Bennington, was a trip without fear. When the first signs for the New York State line appeared, the driver said, 'It's all right.' The Volvo believed him.

It was a dusty tomato-red two-door sedan, 1969, with all-black Semperit radial tires, standard four-speed transmission, four cylinders, two carburetors and 45,238 miles of experience without a radio. It was the driver's feeling that a radio would be distracting to them both.

They had started out at midnight from Vermont. 'Dawn in Pennsylvania!' the driver told the worried Volvo.

*      *      *

In Troy, New York, the driver used steady down-shifting and a caressing voice to reassure the Volvo that all this would soon pass. 'Not much more of this,' he said. The Volvo took him at his word. Sometimes it is necessary to indulge illusions.

At the nearly abandoned entrance to the New York State Thruway, West, an innocent Volkswagen exhibited indecision concerning which lane to use. The driver eased up close behind the Volkswagen and allowed the Volvo's horn to blare; the Volkswagen, near panic, swerved right; the Volvo opened up on the left, passed, cut in with aggression, flashed taillights.

The Volvo felt better.

The New York State Thruway is hours and hours long; the driver knew that monotony is a dangerous thing. He therefore left the Thruway at Syracuse and made an extended detour to Ithaca, driving a loop around Lake Cayuga and meeting up with the Thruway again near Rochester. The countryside bore a comforting resemblance to Vermont. Apples smelled as if they were growing; maple leaves were falling in front of the headlights. Only once was there an encounter with a shocking, night-lit sign which seemed to undermine the Volvo's confidence. LIVE BAIT! the sign said. The driver had troublesome visions with that one himself, but he knew it could be infectious to express his imagination too vividly. 'Just little worms and things,' he said to the Volvo, who purred along. But there lurked in the driver's mind the possibility of *other* kinds of 'live bait' – a kind of reverse-working bait, which rather than luring the fish to nibble would scare them out of the water. Throw in some of this

74

special bait and retrieve the terrified, gasping fish from where they'd land on shore. Or perhaps LIVE BAIT! was the name of a nightclub.

It was actually with relief that the driver returned to the Thruway. Not every excursion from the main road leads one back. But the driver just patted the dashboard and said, 'Pretty soon we'll be in Buffalo.'

A kind of light was in the sky – a phase seen only by duck hunters and marathon lovers. The driver had seen little of that light.

Lake Erie lay as still and gray as a dead ocean; the cars on the Pennsylvania Interstate were just those few early risers who commute to Ohio. 'Don't let Cleveland get you down,' the driver warned.

The Volvo looked superbly fit – tires cool, gas mileage at 22.3 per gallon, oil full up, battery water ample and undisturbed. The only indication that the whole fearsome night had been journeyed was the weird wingmash and blur of bug stains which blotched the windshield and webbed the grille.

The gas-station attendant had to work his squeegee very hard. 'Going a long way?' he asked the driver, but the driver just shrugged. I'm going all the way! he longed to shout, but the Volvo was right there.

You have to watch who you hurt with what you say. For example, the driver hadn't told anyone he was leaving.

They skirted the truck traffic around Cleveland before Cleveland could get them in its foul grasp; they left behind them the feeling that the morning rush hour was angry it just missed them. COLUMBUS, SOUTH, said a sign, but the driver snorted with scorn and sailed up the West ramp of the Ohio Turnpike.

'Crabs in ice water to you, Columbus,' he said.

When you've come through a night of well-controlled tension and you're underway in the morning with that feeling of a head-start advantage on the rest of the world, even Ohio seems possible – even Toledo appears to be just a short sprint away.

'Lunch in Toledo!' the driver announced, with daring. The Volvo gave a slight shudder at seventy-five, skipped to eighty and found that fabled 'second wind'; the sun was behind them and they both relished the Volvo's squat shadow fleeing in front of them. They felt they could follow that vision to Indiana.

Early morning goals are among the illusions we must indulge if we're going to get anywhere at all.

There is more to Ohio than you think; there are more exits to Sandusky than seem reasonable. At one of the many and anonymous rest pavilions off the turnpike, the Volvo had a severe fit of pre-ignition and the driver had to choke off the car's lunging coughs by executing a sharp stallout with the clutch. This irritated them both. And when he made the mileage calculations on the new full tank, the driver was hasty and thoughtless enough to blurt out the disappointing performance. 'Fourteen and six tenths miles a gallon!' Then he quickly tried to make the Volvo know that this wasn't offered as criticism. 'It was that last gas,' he said. 'They gave you some bad gas.'

But the Volvo was slow and wheezing to start; it idled low and stalled pulling away from the pumps, and the driver thought it was best to say, 'Oil's full up, not burning a drop.' This was a lie; the Volvo was down half a quart – not enough to add, but below the mark. For a sickening moment, past one more countless exit for Sandusky, the driver wondered if the Volvo *knew*. For distance, trust is essential. Can a car feel its oil level falling?

'Lunch in Toledo' hulked in the driver's mind like a taunt; lapsed hunger informed him that lunchtime could have been dawdled away at any of fourteen exits which pretended to lead to Sandusky. God, what *was* Sandusky?

The Volvo, though quenched and wiped, had gone without a proper rest since breakfast in Buffalo. The driver decided to let his own lunch pass. 'I'm not hungry,' he said cheerfully, but he felt the weight of his second lie. The driver knew that some sacrifices are tokens. If you're in a thing together, a fair share of the suffering must be a top priority. The area referred to as 'Toledo' was silently passed in the afternoon like an unmentionable anticlimax. And as for the matter of a falling oil level, the driver knew he was down half a quart of his own. Oh, Ohio.

Fort Wayne, Elkhart, Muncie, Gary, Terre Haute and Michigan City – *ah, Indiana!* A different state, not planted with cement. 'Green as Vermont,' the driver whispered. *Vermont!* A magic word. 'Of course, flatter,' he added, then feared he might have said too much.

A drenching, cleansing thunderstorm broke over the Volvo in Lagrange; gas mileage at Goshen read 20.2, a figure the driver chanted to the Volvo like a litany – past Ligonier, past Nappanee. Boring their way into the heartland, the driver sensed the coming on of an unprecedented 'third wind'.

Cows appeared to like Indiana. But what was a 'Hoosier'?

Shall we have supper in South Bend? A punt's

distance from Notre Dame. Nonsense! Gas mileage 23.5! Push on!

Even the motels were appealing; swimming pools winked alongside them. Have a good night's sleep! Indiana seemed to sing.

'Not yet,' the driver said. He had seen the signs for Chicago. To wake up in the morning with Chicago already passed by, successfully avoided, out-maneuvered — what a head start that would be!

At the Illinois line, he figured the time, the distance to Chicago, the coincidence of his arrival with the rush hour, etc. The Volvo's case of pre-ignition was gone; it shut off calmly; it appeared to have mastered the famous 'kiss start'. After the uplift of Indiana, how bad could Illinois be?

'We will be by-passing Chicago at six-thirty p.m.,' the driver said. 'The worst of the rush hour will be over. We'll drive an hour away from Chicago, downstate Illinois — just to get out in the country again — and we'll definitely stop by eight. A wash for you, a swim for me! Mississippi catfish poached in white wine, an Illinois banana boat, a pint of STP, a cognac in the Red Satin Bar, let some air escape from your tires, in bed by ten, cross the Mississippi at first light, breakfast in Iowa, sausage from homegrown hogs, Nebraska by noon, corn fritters for lunch . . .'

He talked the Volvo into it. They drove into what the license plates call 'the Land of Lincoln'.

'Good-bye, Indiana! Thank you, Indiana!' the driver sang from the old tune: *I Wish I Was a Hoosier*, by M. Lampert. We will often do anything to pretend that nothing is on our minds.

Smog bleared the sky ahead, the sun was not down but

it was screened. The highway changed from clear tar to cement slabs with little cracks every second saying, *'Thunk ker-thunk, thunk ker-thunk . . .'* Awful, endless, identical suburbs of outdoor barbecue pits were smoldering.

Nearing the first Chicago interchange, the driver stopped for fresh gas, a look at that falling oil, a pressure check on the tires – just to be sure. The traffic was getting thicker. A transistor radio hung round the gas-station attendant's neck announced that the water temperature in Lake Michigan was seventy-two degrees.

*'Ick!'* the driver said. Then he saw that the clock on the gas pump did not agree with his watch. He had crossed a time zone, somewhere – maybe in that fantasy called Indiana. He was coming into Chicago an hour earlier than he thought: dead-center, rush-hour traffic hurtled past him. Around him now were the kinds of motels where swimming pools were filled with soot. He imagined the cows who could have woken him with their gentle bells, back in good old Indiana. He had been eighteen and a half hours on the road – with only a breakfast in Buffalo to remember.

'One bad mistake every eighteen and a half hours isn't so bad,' he told the Volvo. For optimists, a necessary comeback. And a remarkable bit of repression to think of this mistake as the first.

'Hello, Illinois. Hello to you, half of Chicago.'

The Volvo drank a quart of oil like that first tall Indiana cocktail the driver was dreaming of.

If the driver thought Sandusky was guilty of gross excess, it would be gross excess itself to represent the range of his feelings for Joliet.

Two hours of lane-changing inched him less than

79

thirty miles southwest of Chicago and placed him at the crossroads for the travelers heading west – even to Omaha – and south to St Louis, Memphis and New Orleans. Not to mention errant fools laboring north to Chicago, Milwaukee and Green Bay – and rarer travelers still, seeking Sandusky and the shimmering East.

Joliet, Illinois, was where Chicago parked its trucks at night. Joliet was where people who mistook the Wisconsin interchange for the Missouri interchange discovered their mistake and gave up.

The four four-lane highways that converged on Joliet like mating spiders had spawned two Howard Johnson Motor Lodges, three Holiday Inns and two Great Western Motels. All had indoor swimming pools, air conditioning and color TV. The color TV was an absurd attempt at idealism: to bring color to Joliet, Illinois, an area which was predominantly black and white.

At eight-thirty p.m. the driver resigned from the open road.

'I'm sorry,' he said to the Volvo. There was no car wash at the Holiday Inn. What would have been the point? And it's doubtful that the Volvo heard him, or could have been consoled; the Volvo was suffering from a bout of pre-ignition that lurched and shook the madly clutching driver so badly that he lost all patience.

'Damn car,' he muttered, at an awkward silence – a reprieve in the Volvo's fit. Well, the damage was done. The Volvo just sat there, *pinging* with heat, tires hot and hard, carburetors in hopeless disagreement, plugs caked with carbon, oil filter no doubt choked as tightly closed as a sphincter muscle.

'I'm sorry,' the driver said. 'I didn't mean it. We'll

get off to a fresh start in the morning.'

In the ghastly green-lit lobby, arranged with turtle aquariums and potted palms, the driver encountered about eleven hundred registering travelers, all in a shell-shocked state resembling his own, all telling their children and wives and cars: 'I'm sorry, we'll get off to a fresh start in the morning . . .'

But disbelief was everywhere. When good faith has been violated, we have our work cut out for us.

The driver knew when good faith had been violated. He sat on the industrial double bed in Holiday Inn Rm. 879 and placed a collect phone call to his wife in Vermont.

'Hello, it's me,' he said.

'Where have you *been*?' she cried. 'God, everyone's been looking.'

'I'm sorry,' he told her.

'I looked all around that awful party for you,' she said. 'I was sure you had gone off somewhere with that Helen Cranitz.'

'Oh no.'

'Well, I finally *humiliated* myself by actually finding her . . . she was with Ed Poines.'

'Oh no.'

'And when I saw you'd taken the car I got so worried about what you'd been drinking . . .'

'I was sober.'

'Well, Derek Marshall had to drive me home and he *wasn't*.'

'I'm sorry.'

'Well, nothing *happened*!'

'I'm sorry . . .'

*'Sorry!'* she screamed. 'Where are you? I needed the

car to take Carey to the dentist. I called the police.'

'Oh no.'

'Well, I thought you might be in a ditch somewhere off the road.'

'The car's fine.'

'The *car*!' she wailed. 'Where are you? For God's sake . . .'

'I'm in Joliet, Illinois.'

'I've had more than enough of your terrible humor . . .'

'We screwed up at Chicago or I'd be in Iowa.'

'Who's we?'

'Just me.'

'You said we.'

'I'm sorry . . .'

'I just want to know if you're coming home tonight.'

'It's unlikely I could get there,' the driver said.

'Well, I've got Derek Marshall on my hands again, you can thank yourself for that. He took Carey to the dentist for me.'

'Oh no.'

'He's been a perfect gentleman, of course, but I really had to ask him by. He's worried about you, too, you know.'

'Like hell . . .'

'You're in no position to talk like that to me. When are you coming back?'

The thought of 'coming back' had not occurred to the driver and he was slow to respond.

'I want to know where you are, *really,*' his wife said.

'Joliet, Illinois.'

She hung up.

The longer distances take teamwork. The driver had his work cut out for him, for sure.

*　　*　　*

Bobbing in the indoor pool, the driver was struck with a certain bilious sensation and the resemblance the pool bore to the turtle aquariums in the Holiday Inn lobby. I don't want to be here, he thought.

In the Grape Arbor Restaurant the driver pondered the dizzying menu, then ordered the chef's crab salad. It came. Lake Michigan should be suspected as a possible, ominous source.

In the Tahiti Bar he was served cognac.

The local Joliet TV station reported the highway fatalities of the day: a grim body count – the vision of the carbon-covered carnage sending travelers away from the bar and to bed early, for a night of troubled sleep. Perhaps this was the purpose of the program.

Before he went to bed himself, the driver said goodnight to his Volvo. He felt its tires, he felt the black grit in the oil, he sought the degree of damage in a pockmark on the windshield.

'That one must have stung.'

*Derek Marshall!* That one stung, too.

The driver remembered what has been referred to as 'that awful party'. He told his wife he was going to the bathroom; cars were parked all over the lawn and he went to the bathroom there. Little Carey was staying at a friend's house; there was no babysitter to see the driver slip home for his toothbrush.

A dress of his wife's, a favorite one of his, hung on the back of the bathroom door. He nuzzled it; he grew fainthearted at its silky feel: his tire gauge snagged on the zipper as he tried to pull away from it. 'Goodbye,' he told the dress, firmly.

For a rash moment he considered taking all her

83

clothes with him! But it was midnight – time for turning to pumpkin – and he sought the Volvo.

His wife was a dusty tomato-red . . . no. She was blond, seven years married with one child and without a radio. A radio was distracting to them both. No. His wife took a size-10 dress, wore out three pairs of size-7 sandals between spring and fall, used a 36B bra and averaged 23.4 miles per gallon . . . *no!* She was a small dark person with strong fingers and intense sea-blue eyes like airmail envelopes; she had the habit of putting her head back like a wrestler about to bridge or a patient preparing for mouth-to-mouth resuscitation whenever she made love . . . oh yes. She had a svelte, not a voluptuous, body and she liked things that clung to her, hugged her, hung around her . . . clothes, children, big dogs and men. She was tall with long thighs and a loping walk, a great mouth, a 38D . . .

Then the driver's sinuses finally revolted against the night-long endurance test forced upon them by the air conditioning; he sneezed violently and woke himself up. He put his thoughts for his wife and all other women in a large, empty part of his mind which resembled the Volvo's roomy, unpacked trunk. He took a forceful shower and thought that today was the day he would see the Mississippi.

People actually learn very little about themselves; it's as if they really appreciate the continuous act of making themselves vulnerable.

The driver planned to leave without breakfast. You'd have thought he'd be used to ups and downs, but the early morning sight of the violence done to the Volvo was a shock even to this veteran of the ways of the road. The Volvo had been vandalized. It sat at the curb by the driver's motel room like a wife he'd locked out of the house in the drunken night – she was waiting there to hit him hard with his guilt in the daylight.

'Oh my God, what have they done to you . . . ?'

They had pried off the four hubcaps and left the cluster of tire nuts exposed, the tires naked. They had stolen the side-view mirror from the driver's side. Someone had tried to unscrew the whole mounting for the piece, but the screwdriver had been either too big or too small for the screws; the work had left the screwheads maimed and useless; the thief had left the mounting in place and simply wrenched the mirror until it had snapped free at the ball joint. The ruptured joint looked to the driver like the raw and ragged socket of a man whose arm had been torn off.

They had tried to violate the Volvo's interior with repeated digging and levering at the sidevent windows, but the Volvo had held. They had ripped the rubber water seal from under the window on the driver's side but they had not been able to spring the lock. They had tried to break one window: a small run of cracks, like a spider web blown against the glass, traced a pattern on the passenger's side. They had tried to get into the gas tank – to siphon gas, to add sand, to insert a match – but although they had mashed the tank-top lock, they had been unable to penetrate there. They had cranked under the hood, but the hood had held. Several teeth of the grille were pushed in, and one tooth had been bent outward until it had broken; it stuck out in front of the Volvo as if the car were carrying some crude bayonet.

As a last gesture, the frustrated rapists, the wretched band of Joliet punks – or were they other motel guests, irritated by the foreign license plate, in disagreement with Vermont? . . . whoever, as a finally cruel and needless way of leaving, *someone* had taken an instrument (the corkscrew blade on a camper's knife?) and gouged a four-letter word into the lush red of the Volvo's hood. Indeed, deeper than the paint, it was a groove into the steel itself. SUCK was the word.

'Suck?' the driver cried out. He covered the wound with his hand. 'Bastards!' he screamed. 'Swine, filthy creeps!' he roared. The wing of the motel he was facing must have slept two hundred travelers; there was a ground-floor barracks and a second-floor barracks with a balcony. 'Cowards, car-humpers!' the driver bellowed. 'Who did it?' he demanded. Several doors along the balcony opened. Frightened, wakened men stood peering down at him – women chattering behind them: 'Who is it? What's happening?'

'Suck!' the driver yelled. 'Suck!'

'It's six o'clock in the morning, fella,' someone mumbled from a ground-floor door, then quickly stepped back inside and closed the door behind him.

Genuine madness is not to be tampered with. If the driver had been drunk or simply boorish, those disturbed sleepers would have mangled him. But he was insane – they could all see – and there's nothing to do about that.

'What's going on, Fred?'

'Some guy losing his mind. Go back to sleep.'

Oh Joliet, Illinois, you are worse than the purgatory I first took you for!

The driver touched the oily ball joint where his trim mirror used to be. 'You're going to be all right,' he said. 'Good as new, don't worry.'

86

S U C K! That foul word dug into his hood was *so public* it seemed to expose him – the rude, leering ugliness of it shamed him. He saw Derek Marshall approaching his wife. 'Hi! Need a ride home?'

'All right,' the driver told the Volvo, thickly. 'All right, that's enough. I'll take you home.'

The gentleness of the driver was now impressive. It is incredible to find occasional discretion in human beings; some of the people on the second-floor balcony were actually closing their doors. The driver's hand hid the SUCK carved into his hood; he was crying. He had come all this way to leave his wife and all he had done was hurt his car.

But no-one can make it as far as Joliet, Illinois, and not be tempted to see the Mississippi River – the main street of the Midwest, and the necessary crossing to the real Outwest. No, you haven't really been West until you've crossed the Mississippi; you can never say you've 'been out there' until you've touched down in Iowa. If you have seen Iowa, you have seen the beginning.

The driver *knew* this; he begged the Volvo to indulge him just a look. 'We'll turn right around. I promise. I just want to see it,' he said. 'The Mississippi. And Iowa . . .' where he might have gone.

Sullenly, the Volvo carried him through Illinois: Starved Rock State Park, Wenona, Mendota, Henry, Kewanee, Geneseo, Rock Island and Moline. There was a rest plaza before the great bridge which spanned the Mississippi -- the bridge which carried you into Iowa. Ah, Davenport, West Liberty and Lake MacBride!

But he would not see them, not now. He stood by the Volvo and watched the tea-coloured, wide water of the Mississippi roll by; for someone who's seen the Atlantic Ocean, rivers aren't so special. But *beyond* the river ... there was *Iowa* ... and it looked really *different* from Illinois! He saw corn tassels going on forever, like an army of fresh young cheerleaders waving their feathers. Out there, too, big hogs grew; he knew that; he imagined them – he had to – because there wasn't actually a herd of pigs browsing on the other side of the Mississippi.

'Some day . . .' the driver said, half in fear that this was true and half wishfully. The compromised Volvo sat there waiting for him; its bashed grille and the word SUCK pointed east.

'Okay, okay,' the driver said.

Be thankful for what dim orientation you have. Listen: the driver *could* have gotten lost; in the muddle of his east–west decision, he could have headed north – in the southbound lane!

Missouri State Police Report # 459: 'A red Volvo sedan, heading north in the southbound lane, appeared to have a poor sense of direction. The cement mixer who hit him was absolutely clear about its right-of-way in the passing lane. When the debris was sorted, a phone number was found. When his wife was called, another man answered. He said his name was Derek Marshall and that he'd give the news to the guy's wife as soon as she woke up.'

We should know: it can always be worse.

Certainly, real trouble lay ahead. There was the complexity of the Sandusky exits to navigate, and the driver felt less than fresh. Ohio lay out there, waiting for him like years of a marriage he hadn't yet lived. But there was also the Volvo to think of; the Volvo seemed destined to never get over Vermont. And there would be delicate dealings to come with Derek Marshall; that seemed sure. We often need to lose sight of our priorities in order to see them.

He had seen the Mississippi and the lush, fertile flatland beyond. Who could say what sweet, dark mysteries Iowa might have revealed to him? Not to mention Nebraska. Or *Wyoming*! The driver's throat ached. And he had overlooked that he once more had to pass through Joliet, Illinois.

Going home is hard. But what's to be said for staying away?

In La Salle, Illinois, the driver had the Volvo checked over. The windshield wipers had to be replaced (he hadn't even noticed they were stolen), a temporary side-view mirror was mounted and some soothing anti-rust primer was painted into the gash which said SUCK. The Volvo's oil was full up, but the driver discovered that the vandals had tried to jam little pebbles in all the air valves – hoping to deflate his tires as he drove. The gas-station attendant had to break the tank-top lock the rest of the way in order to give the Volvo some gas. Mileage 23.1 per gallon – the Volvo was a tiger in the face of hardship.

'I'll get you a paint job at home,' the driver told the Volvo, grimly. 'Just try to hang on.'

There was, after all, Indiana to look forward to. Some things, we're told, are even better 'the second time around'. His marriage struck him as an unfinished war between Ohio and Indiana – a fragile balance of firepower, punctuated with occasional treaties. To bring Iowa into the picture would cause a drastic tilt. Or: some rivers are better not crossed? The national average is less than 25,000 miles on one set of tires and many fall off much sooner. He had 46,251 miles on the Volvo – his first set of tires.

No, despite that enchanting, retreating portrait of the Iowa future, you cannot drive with your eyes in the rear-view mirror. And, yes, at this phase of the journey, the driver was determined to head back east. But dignity is difficult to maintain. Stamina requires constant upkeep. Repetition is boring. And you pay for grace.

# WEARY KINGDOM

Minna Barrett, fifty-five, looks precisely as old as she is, and her figure suggests nothing of what she might have looked like 'in her time'. One would only assume that always she looked this way, slightly oblong, gently rounded, not puritanical but almost asexual. A pleasant old maid since grammar school, neat and silent; a not overly stern face, a not overly harsh mouth, but a total composure which now, at fifty-five, reflects the history of her many indifferences and the conservative going of her own way.

Minna has her own room in a dormitory of Fairchild Junior College for Young Women, where she is the matron of the dormitory's small dining hall, in charge of the small kitchen crew, responsible for the appropriate dress of the girls at mealtime. Minna's room has a private entrance and a private bath, is shaded in the mornings by the elms of the campus, and is several blocks from Boston Common – not too far for her to walk on a nice day. This room is remarkably uncluttered, remarkable because it's a very small room which shows very little of the nine years she has lived there. Not that there is, or should be, a great deal to show; it is only as permanent a residence as any other place Minna has lived since she left home. This room has a television and Minna stays up at night, watching the movies. She never watches the regular programs; she reads until the news at eleven. She likes biographies, prefers these to autobiographies, because someone's account of their own life embarrasses her in a way she doesn't understand. She is partial to the biographies of women, although she does read Ian Fleming. Once at a party for the alumnae and trustees of the school, someone, a lady in a soft lavender suit who wanted, she said, to meet *all* of the school's personnel, found out about Minna's interest in biographies. The lavender lady recommended a book by Gertrude Stein, which Minna bought and never finished. It wasn't anything Minna would have called a biography, but she wasn't offended by it. She just felt that nothing ever happened.

So Minna reads until eleven, then watches the news and a movie. The kitchen crew comes early in the morning, but Minna doesn't have to be in the dining hall until the girls come in. After breakfast she takes a cup of coffee to her own room, then maybe naps until lunch. Her afternoons, too, are quiet. Some of the girls in the dormitory will visit her at eleven, to watch the evening news – there is an entrance to Minna's room from the dormitory corridor. The girls probably come to see the television more than they come to see Minna, although they are very pleasant and Minna is amused at the varying stages of their undress at this hour. Once they were interested in how long Minna's hair would be if she let it down. She obliged them, unwinding, unfurling the long gray hair – somewhat stiff, but falling to her hips. The girls were impressed with how thick and healthy it was; one of the girls, with hair almost that long, suggested to Minna that she wear it in a braid. The next evening the girls brought a deep orange ribbon and they braided Minna's hair. Minna was meekly pleased, but she said that she never could wear it that way. She still might be tempted, the girls were so impressed, but it is too much to think of changing her hair from the tightly wrapped bun it has been all these years.

After the girls leave, after the movie, Minna sits in her bed, thinking of her retirement. The farm where she grew up, in South Byfield, comes back to her mind. If she thinks of it with a certain nostalgia she is not aware of this; she thinks only how much more restful her work at the school is, how much easier than on the farm. Her younger brother lives there now, and in a few years she'll return, to live with her brother's family, taking her tidy nest egg with her, and relinquishing herself and her savings to the care of her brother. It was only last Christmas, when she was visiting his family, that they asked her when she would come to stay for good. By the time she feels it is right for her to come, in another year or so, not *all* of her brother's children will be grown-up, and there will be things for her to do. Certainly, no-one would think of Minna as an imposition.

She thinks of South Byfield, what past and what future – after the news, after the movie – and she feels, now, no resentment toward this present time. She has no memories of a painful loss or separation, or failure. There were friends in South Byfield, whom she simply saw married or who just remained there after she quietly moved the thirty miles to Boston; her mother and father died, almost shyly, but there is nothing that she misses with particular pain. She doesn't think of herself as very anxious to retire, although she does look ahead to being a part of her brother's healthy family. She wouldn't say that she has a lot of friends in Boston, but friends for Minna always have been the pleasant and familiar people connected with the regular episodes of her life; they never have been emotional dependents. Now, for example, there is Flynn, the cook, who is Irish with a large family in South Boston, who complains to Minna of Boston housing, Boston traffic, Boston corruption, Boston this-and-that. Minna knows little of this but she listens pleasantly to him; in his swearing Flynn reminds her of her father. Minna doesn't swear herself, but she doesn't find Flynn's swearing unpleasant. He has a way of coaxing things that makes her feel as if his swearing really *works*. The daily battles with the coffee urn are invariably won by Flynn, who after long and dark curses, heavy jostles and violent threats of dismantling the whole thing, emerges the victor; for Minna, Flynn's animated obscenities seem constructive, the way her father would shout the tractor into starting, during the winter months, and Minna thinks Flynn is nice.

Also, there is Mrs Elwood, a widow, with deeper lines on her face than Minna has — lines which move like rubber bands when Mrs Elwood talks, as if her chin were hinged to these lines. Mrs Elwood is the housemother of the dormitory, and she speaks with a British accent; it is well-known that Mrs Elwood is a Bostonian, but she spent one summer in England, after her graduation from college. Apparently, she had a whale of a time there. Minna tells Mrs Elwood whenever there's a movie with Alec Guinness on the late show, and Mrs Elwood comes, discreetly after the news, after her girls have gone back to their rooms. It often takes a good half of the movie for Mrs Elwood to remember if she's seen this one before.

'I must have seen them all, Minna,' Mrs Elwood says.

'I always miss the ones at Christmas time,' Minna replies. 'At my brother's we usually play cards or have folks in.'

'Oh, Minna,' Mrs Elwood says, 'you really should go out more.'

And, too, there is Angelo Gianni. Angelo is pale and slight, a bewildered-looking man, or boy, gray eyes that are merely a deeper shade of the color of his face, and there is nothing about him, outside of his name, to suggest that he's Italian. If his name were Cuthbert, or Cadwallader, there would be nothing in his appearance to suggest that. If he were a Devereaux or a Hunt-Jones you would see nothing of that in his awkward, embarrassed body – anticipating, with awe, the most minor crisis, and reacting dumb-struck every time. Angelo could be twenty or thirty; he lives in the basement of the dormitory, next to his janitor's closet. Angelo empties ashtrays, washes dishes, sets and cleans tables, sweeps, does things like that wherever he is needed, and does other, more complicated things when he is asked, and when the problem has been thoroughly explained to him, more than once. He is exceptionally gentle, and he behaves toward Minna with a curious combination of the deepest respect – at times, calling her 'Miss Minna' – and the odd, shy, flirtatious gestures of true affection. Minna likes Angelo, she is tender and cheerful with him as she is with her brother's children, and she is aware of even *worrying* about him. Angelo, she feels, stands on precarious ground, and at every moment of his simple, delicate life – unguarded, she thinks – he is prone to the cruelest of injuries. The injuries go unnamed, yet Minna can picture a hoard of sufferings lying in wait for Angelo, who lives fragilely, artlessly, in his isolated world of kindness and faith. Minna seeks to protect Angelo, seeks to instruct him, although these sufferings she envisions for him are quite nebulous to her; she can think of no great injury she has received, no great threatening and destructive force which ever has loomed over her. Yet, for Angelo, she fears this, and she tells him her instructive stories, inevitably ending in a proverb (one of those proverbs she cuts from the daily newspaper and pins with a small, uncolored tack to the thick, black pages of her photograph album, which contains only two photographs – one brownish print of her parents, stonily posed, and one color shot of her brother's children). Minna's stories are her own, stripped of any prelude, stripped of time and place, even names of characters, and certainly stripped of any emotional involvement of her own, that might have existed at the time, might linger still – *might,* if Minna ever remembered anything in that way, or if anything could affect her, personally, in that way. The proverbs range from 'A little knowledge is a dangerous thing!' to a whole assembly of mottoes urging compromise. The danger of trusting *too* much, of believing *too* much. Angelo nods to her advice; a frequent, awesome seriousness seems to fix his eyes, suspend his mouth, until Minna is bothered so much by Angelo's painful concentration that she tells him, as a footnote, not to take anything that anyone says too seriously. This only further puzzles Angelo, and seeing what effect she has had, Minna changes the subject to something lighter.

'Why the other day,' she says, 'some of the girls tried to get me to wear my hair in a braid, a long braid.'

'I'll bet you looked nice,' Angelo tells her.

'Oh, you know, Angelo, I just didn't see the good in changing my hair from what it's been so long.'

'You should do what you think best, Miss Minna,' Angelo says, and Minna is helpless to break the penetrating and dangerous kindness which Angelo bears to everyone, bringing them the burden of his exposed heart, to do with as they may. And, well, Minna thinks, it's time they were both back to work.

Minna has no complaints about her work. She has asked for another woman to help her, another matron for the dining hall – so that when Minna has her day off, on Mondays, the girls and the kitchen crew won't be alone. No-one, apparently, regards this request as very important. Mrs Elwood thought it would be a fine idea, said she'd speak to the Director of Housing. Then later, when Minna asked her about it, Mrs Elwood said that she thought it might be better if Minna spoke to the Director, or to someone, herself. Minna wrote to the Director, weeks ago, and she has heard nothing. It's not really important, she thinks, and so there's nothing to complain about. It would just be nice to have another woman, an older woman, of course, and who's had some experience with young girls. There's even an extra room in the dormitory for her, if the college could find a woman like that, who'd like a room of her own – a free room, after all, and all the protection a woman living alone could ask for. It would be nice, to have someone like that, but Minna doesn't push it. She is content to wait.

The first, bored ducks were roaming about as Minna, on her day off, walked through Boston Common. She shawled and unshawled as she walked, warm and then shivering, regarded the optimists in their short-sleeved shirts, their chilly seersucker. Several worldly mallards strutted with the awkward and stunned dignity of someone who'd been conspicuously insulted at a large, unfamiliar party. Shopping, summery mothers with winter-bundled children, blustering in the short blasts of cold wind, paused to find something to feed the ducks. The children leaned out too far, got wet feet, were scolded, hurried and dragged along, looking over their shoulders at the floating pieces of bread and the indifferent ducks. The ducks would get better about this as the spring wore on, but now, in the early stages of their hopeless revolution for privacy, they refused to eat if they were watched. Old men in year-round overcoats, clutching papers and knobby loaves of Jewish bread, hurled heavy chunks to the ducks — the men looked cautiously about, to see if anyone noticed that the pieces were too big (intended to hit and sink the ducks). Minna was cooly aware of their feeble arms and their bad aim. She didn't stay long, but turned out of the Common to Boylston Street. She window-shopped at Shreve's, warming herself in the elegance of crystal and silver, thinking what would be the loveliest piece for her brother's table. Schraft's was around the corner and she ate a small lunch there. Outside of Schraft's she pondered what to do next; it was two o'clock and the weather was typically, indecisively March. Then Minna saw a girl come out of Shreve's, the girl smiled in Minna's direction — a denim skirt came above her knees, sandals, a green, crew-neck sweater, obviously some boy's. The sweater hung low on her hips, the cuffs were rolled, and the stretched knobs on the sleeves, which would have been

100

the boy's elbows, swung like goiters under the girl's slender wrists. She called, 'Hi, Minna!' and Minna recognized her as one of the girls who came to watch the news in her room. Not remembering her name, names always bothered her, Minna called the girl 'Dear'. Dear was going to Cambridge, taking the MTA, wanted to know if Minna would like to come and browse the shops. They went together, Minna greatly pleased at this; she noticed how differently people watched her on the subway – did they think she was this girl's grandmother, or, even, her mother? The smiles were for having such a pretty companion, and Minna felt as if she was being congratulated. In Cambridge they stopped at an extraordinary little delicatessen, where Minna bought several cans of exotic food, the labels in some foreign language, sealed with precious-looking stamps. It was like receiving some gift package from an imaginary uncle, a world traveler, adventurer sort. In a dusty little shop of orange crates and awnings, a shop with a lot of dulled and dented pewter, Minna bought a silver hors d'oeuvre fork, with which, the girl called 'Dear' told her, she could comfortably eat the exotic foods. The girl was very kind to Minna, so kind that Minna felt she must not be well-liked by the other girls. At four o'clock the day turned ragged and cold once more, and the two of them went to a foreign movie in Brattle Square. They had to sit quite close to the front because Minna had difficulty reading the subtitles. Minna was embarrassed that the girl should see this film, but later the girl spoke so knowingly and seriously about it that Minna was somewhat eased. They had a nice meal after the movie – dark beer, sauerkraut and stuffed peppers, in a German restaurant that the girl knew well. The girl told Minna that they wouldn't have served her the beer if Minna hadn't been with her. It was well after dark when they returned to the dormitory, and Minna told the girl what a lovely time she'd had. With her little bag of funny foods and the hors d'oeuvre fork, and feeling pleasantly tired, Minna went to her room. Although it was only nine o'clock she felt she could go to bed right away, but on her desk where she gently set her bag, she saw a curious, beige folder with a note attached. The note was from Mrs Elwood.

Dear Minna, I dropped this in your room this afternoon. The Director of Housing called me this morning to say that he'd found you a helper, another matron for the dining hall, and *with* experience. The Director said he was sending her over here. Since you were out I showed her around, got her settled in her room – it's a bit of a shame that she has to share the bathroom with the girls on that floor, but she did seem quite pleased with everything. She's most attractive – Angelo seems rather taken with her – and I told her that you'd take care of her in the morning. If you want to go and meet her tonight, she said she was tired, she'll be in her room.

So, Minna thought, they really got someone. She couldn't imagine what might be in the folder, and opening it, delicately, she saw it was a duplicate of the woman's job application. She felt a little uncertain about looking at this, it appeared to be such a private thing, but her eye caught the little bag of worldly foods and this, somehow, gave her confidence to read the application. Celeste was her name and she was forty-one. She'd done a 'lot of waiting-on table', had been a counselor at a summer camp for girls, and she was from Heron's Neck, Maine – where her brother-in-law now operated an inn for summer tourists. She had also worked there. The inn had been owned by her parents. It sounds very nice, Minna thought, and she forgot how tired she had been. She suddenly became organized – arranging, proudly, the little cans of the curious food on the overhanging shelf of her desk. Then she checked the TV bulletin to see if there was an Alec Guinness movie on the late show. Mrs Elwood would like to know, and the new woman might be lonely. Indeed, on this most surprising day, there was an Alec Guinness movie. Minna opened the door to the dormitory corridor and walked humming to Celeste's room. She thought, what a wonderful day it's been. She only wished she knew that Dear Girl's name, but she could ask Mrs Elwood about that.

Minna rapped lightly on Celeste's door and heard, or thought she heard a murmured 'Come in.' She opened the door, hesitating on the threshold because the room was dark – all dark, except for the wobbly-necked desk lamp which pointed its feeble light to the cushion of the desk chair. The room, like most end-rooms in dormitories, was neither square nor rectangular. Any symmetry appeared as an accident; there were *five* corners where the ceiling sloped almost to the floor, and several alcoves in juxtaposition to the corners. In one of those low-ceilinged alcoves was the bed, a cot really, and Minna saw that some attempt had been made to conceal the bed from the rest of the room. A heavy, crimson blanket was draped from the molding and hung in such a way as to wall-off the bed in the alcove. Minna saw the blanket flap and she guessed there was a window open over the bed. The whole room was somewhat windy in the early evening cool, yet the room smelled of a heavy, animal musk, rich as coffee, and reminded Minna – oddly, she thought – of one late evening last summer when her brother had been in Boston and had taken her to a show. They were riding back on the subway, alone in the car, when a massive Negress in a gaudy, flowered dress came in and sat just a few seats away. The Negress had stepped in from the steamy rain, the damp underground, and suddenly the car was filled with this rich scent – smells of a hot summer day in a dirt floor cellar, closed all winter with its jams and pickled beans. Minna whispered, 'Celeste?' – heard another murmur from behind the crimson blanket, was aware of the odor again, somehow arousing and malign. Minna gently pulled back a corner of the blanket; the faint light from the desk lamp dully illuminated the long, large body of Celeste in a weird sleep. The pillow rested under her shoulder blades, tipping her head back and stretching a long, graceful neck – graceful, despite a sinewy muscled look, visible in the swollen cords which even in the poor light Minna could trace to the high, arched collar bones and chest. Her breasts were rigid, full and not sagging, not fallen to her armpits. Minna saw, only with this observation of the breasts, that Celeste was naked. Her hips were hugely broad, flat dents lay inside her pelvis, neatly symmetrical, and despite a certain heaviness to every part of her body – a forceful, peasant weight to her ankles, a rounded smoothness in her thighs – the length of Celeste's waist, the incredible length of her legs, made her appear almost slender. Minna spoke to her again, louder this time, and then, as soon as she heard her own voice, wished she hadn't said anything

104

– thinking, how awful it would be if the poor woman woke up and saw *me* here. Yet, Minna didn't leave. This terrible body – terrible, in its intimate potential for strength and motion – fixed Minna to the bedside. Now Celeste began to move, slightly, first her hands. The broad, flat fingers curled, her hands cupped, as if to hold some tiny, wounded animal. Then her hands turned palms-down on the bed and her fingers picked at the folds and wrinkles in the sheet. Minna wanted to reach out and calm the hands, fearing they would wake Celeste, but her own hands, her whole body, felt frozen. Celeste turned on one elbow, arched her back, and the hands fell with a soft plop on her wide, flat stomach. Slowly and lightly at first, then with more weight and force, pressing with the heels of her hands, Celeste rubbed her stomach. The hands moved into the flat hollows of her pelvis, rolled the loose, puppy-like skin; the hands pulled down on the hips, pulled away from the waist, turned under the thighs – up, beneath the buttocks, up, to the small of the back. Celeste lifted herself, arched her back again, higher; her great neck cords thickened, empurpled by this exertion, and her mouth – slack, only a moment ago – curled up at the corners to a senseless grin. Celeste opened her eyes, blinked, saw nothing (Minna saw nothing but whites), and then Celeste's eyes closed. Her whole body now softly relaxed, appeared to sink deeply into the bed, and into a truer sleep; the long, still hands rested lightly inside her thighs. Minna backed out of the alcove, noticed the desk lamp, turned it off. Then she left, careful not to let the door bang behind her.

Back in her room, the bright cans of happy food smiled at Minna from her desk. Minna sat and looked at them. She felt strangely exhausted, and it would have been so nice for Mrs Elwood and Celeste to join her for the movie – dining, exquisitely, out of the gay cans. But then, there wouldn't have been enough hors d'oeuvre forks to go around. Even if Mrs Elwood came alone there wouldn't be a fork for her – and, Minna thought, I don't have a can opener. She had to tell Mrs Elwood about the movie, too, and she felt again the strange exhaustion, just sitting where she was. Celeste, Minna thought, certainly *looked* a lot younger than forty-one. Of course the light had been poor, and in sleep the crowsfeet always are softened and smoothed. But, she hadn't been *really* asleep. It hadn't looked, to Minna, *quite* like a dream. And how black her hair was! Perhaps it was dyed. Poor thing, she must have been very tired, or upset. Still, Minna couldn't escape the embarrassment of it! It was a little like reading one of the autobiographies. Embarrassment, for Minna, was a general feeling she experienced often for others, almost never for herself; there didn't seem to be different *kinds* of embarrassment, and the degree to which Minna felt embarrassed could be measured only by how long the feeling lasted.

Well, there were all these things to be done and she'd better get at them. First, Mrs Elwood and the movie. Another fork and a can opener. She would ask Mrs Elwood about that Dear Girl, and find out her name. But Mrs Elwood would surely ask Minna about Celeste, had Minna gone to meet her? – and *what* would she say? Why, yes, she'd gone to meet her, but the poor woman was asleep. Then Celeste would know she'd been there; and the desk lamp, Minna shouldn't have turned it off. She should have left everything as it was. Minna thought, for one wild moment, that she could go back to Celeste's room, turn on the lamp. Then she thought, What nonsense! Celeste had been asleep – not aware, in her sleep, of anything Minna might have seen. Except, of course, that she was naked, and she would certainly know she'd been naked. Well, what of it? Celeste wouldn't care about that. And Minna suddenly realized that she was thinking she already *knew* Celeste; she couldn't get that idea out of her mind. It seemed that she *did* know her, and how silly that was. Knowing someone, for Minna, was a matter of long, slow familiarity. Why that girl, for instance, with whom she'd spent such a delightful afternoon – Minna didn't *know* her at all.

Again, cheerily, the cans on Minna's desk hailed her. But there came, too, the curious exhaustion. If she didn't tell Mrs Elwood about the movie she could go to bed right now; of course, there would have to be a note on the door to tell the girls, No News Tonight. But the thought of bed seemed not quite what her exhaustion asked of her; in fact going to bed was out of the question. Mrs Elwood enjoys the Alec Guinness movies so much, Minna thought, How could I think of such a thing? She looked at the cans again, and there was something about the foreignness of the little colored labels that repulsed her. Then someone knocked on the door, two raps, and Minna was startled – as if, it struck her, she'd been caught doing something wrong.

'Minna? Minna, are you in?' It was Mrs Elwood. Minna opened the door, too slowly, too cautiously, and she saw Mrs Elwood's puzzled face.

'My word, Minna, were you in bed?'

'Oh, no!' Minna cried.

Mrs Elwood came in and said, 'Lord, how dark it is in here!' and Minna noticed that she hadn't turned on the overheads. Only her desk lamp was on – a single, unsteady shaft of light which illuminated the gaudy foods.

'Oh, what are these?' Mrs Elwood asked, moving warily to the desk.

'I had the nicest afternoon,' Minna said. 'I met one of the girls downtown and we went to Cambridge together, shopping, and we saw a movie and ate in a German place. I only got back a moment ago. Or, maybe, twenty minutes.'

'I'd say it was more like twenty minutes,' Mrs Elwood said. 'I saw you both come in.'

'Oh, then you saw her. What *is* her name?'

'You spent the afternoon with her and you don't know her name?'

'I should have known it, really. She watches television. I just would have felt foolish to ask.'

'Lord, Minna!' Mrs Elwood said. 'The girl is Molly Cabot, and she seems to spend more time shopping and movie-going than she does in her classes.'

'Oh, she was so nice to me,' Minna said. 'I didn't think about her classes, she was such a sweet girl. I *did* think she was lonely. But she's not in any trouble, is she?'

'Well, trouble,' Mrs Elwood repeated, turning one of the strange cans in her hand, scrutinizing the label and setting the can back in the row with a disapproving scowl. 'I should say she's in trouble if she doesn't start going to her classes.'

'Oh, I'm so sorry,' Minna said. 'She was so nice. I had a lovely day.'

'Well,' Mrs Elwood said toughly, 'perhaps she'll pull herself together.'

Minna nodded, feeling sad, wishing she could help. Mrs Elwood was still looking at the cans, and Minna hoped that she wouldn't notice the extravagant hors d'oeuvre fork.

'What's *in* these things?' Mrs Elwood asked, holding another can in her lumpy palm.

'They're delicacies from other countries. Molly said they were very good.'

'I wouldn't buy anything to *eat* if I didn't know what it was,' Mrs Elwood said. 'Lord, they might be *unclean*! They might be from *Italy,* or somewhere like that.'

'Oh, I just thought they were pretty,' Minna said, and the familiar exhaustion seemed to numb her whole body and her speech. 'It was a pleasant way to spend the afternoon,' she mumbled, and there was something bitter which came into her voice and surprised her, surprised Mrs Elwood, too, and brought an unsettling quiet to the small room.

'I think you're very tired,' Mrs Elwood said. 'Let me put a note up for the girls, and you go to bed.' The authority of Mrs Elwood's voice seemed to fill Minna's exhaustion, so perfectly, and it made unnecessary any protest. Minna didn't even mention the Alec Guinness movie.

But her sleep was bothered by vague phantoms, in conspiracy, it seemed, with the occasional scratching in the dormitory corridor – presumably the girls who came to see the news and shuffled, puzzled, around the note on the door. Once Minna was sure that Celeste was in the room, still awesomely naked and huge, surrounded by grotesque dwarfs – like those horrific snail-men and fish-people, sub-human crustaceans, Silurian-old, dreamily emerged from a Breughel or a Bosch. Once Minna woke, felt the warm weight of her tired hands against her sides, and felt repelled by her own touch. She lay back again, her arms outstretched to the sides of her bed, her fingers curled beneath the mattress as if she were manacled to a rack. If Minna had eaten one of the strange foods, which she had not, she would have attributed her nightmares to this. But as it was, inexplicable, her troubled sleep struck her as somewhat of an enigma.

If Minna had any recurrent flickers of embarrassment, any lasting reservations regarding Celeste, nothing of the kind was at all apparent. If she was envious of Celeste's easy vibrancy – her immediate intimacy with the girls, with gruff Flynn, especially with Angelo – she wasn't conscious of such an envy. In fact, it was not until several weeks after the first, awful night that Minna recalled how Mrs Elwood had not even *asked* her if she'd gone to meet Celeste. Also, Minna had occasion to see more of Molly Cabot, she felt obligated to see more of her, to mother her, in some small, inoffensive way; but Minna's sense of duty took none of the former pleasures away from Molly's company. Minna enjoyed the shy, secretive closeness of her days with Molly. As she saw more of Molly, she saw less of Angelo – not that she stopped worrying about him. Angelo, as Mrs Elwood had said, was 'rather taken with' Celeste. He brought her flowers – expensive, gaudy and tasteless flowers, which he couldn't have stolen in the Common but would have had to buy. And Celeste received other, less open admiration. On Saturdays the girls were allowed to bring their weekend dates to the dining hall for lunch, and Celeste certainly was noticed. The looks which the boys gave her were seldom casual; they were the penetrating weighted looks which Celeste, when her head was turned, received from Flynn – darkly and stealthily watching her from behind various pots and counters. Minna, if she thought anything of this, thought it rather unbecoming to Flynn, and simply rude of the boys. If she worried about Angelo's adoration, she thought of it as nothing more than another example of Angelo's tragic exposure of himself. Celeste, certainly, offered no threat to Angelo. Angelo, as before, simply was a threat to himself.

Minna was perfectly at ease with Celeste. In two months Celeste had made herself at home; she was gay, a little raucous, always pleasant. The girls were obviously impressed with (or envious of) what Molly called 'her Modigliani allure,' and Flynn appeared to get great pleasure from his dark observations. Mrs Elwood thought Celeste was charming, even if a bit bold. Minna liked her.

In June, with only a few weeks of regular classes remaining, Celeste bought an old car – a dented relic of Boston traffic. Once she drove Minna and Molly Cabot to Cambridge, for an afternoon's shopping. The car smelled of sun-tan oil and cigarettes – and, Minna noticed – of the curious, heavy scent, coffee-rich, the musk of sheeted furniture in unattended summer homes. Celeste drove like a man, one arm out the window, forceful wrenches on the wheel, fond of shifting from third to second, fond of competing with taxis. The car labored and knocked with sudden acceleration; Celeste explained that the carburetor was dirty or ill-adjusted. Minna and Molly nodded their bewildered respect. Celeste took her days off at Revere Beach; she became deeply tanned but complained about the 'pee-like' condition of the water. It was an eager and active time of year.

And June brought a certain impatience to the girls, an irritable quality to Flynn, who always was great at sweating but seemed to suffer most acutely from this in Boston's early and long summers. Minna had grown quite used to the heat, it didn't seem to bother her much, and she noticed that she rarely sweated anymore. Angelo, of course, was forever pale and dry, a completely aseasonal face and body. Celeste looked damply hot.

June was an almost-over time of year, when the girls were brighter and more often in handsome company, when the weekend dining hall was something like a restless, overly-chaperoned party. In a while, there would be different girls in the dormitory for the summer session, and summer sessions were so different anyway, lighter, breezier – and from the kitchen's point of view, people ate less. Now there was a distinctly light-handed way about things. Angelo, during the presentation of one horrendous bouquet to Celeste, asked her to see a movie with him. Their heads struggled on either side of the flowers, Angelo peering for an answer, Celeste amused, both at the size of the bouquet and at Angelo's question.

'What movie is it, Angelo?' Her wide, strong mouth; her rich, good teeth.

'Oh, some movie. We'll have to find one close. I don't have a car.'

'Then sometime let's go in mine,' Celeste said. And then, looking at the ridiculous bouquet, 'Where on earth shall we put this? – by the window, out of Flynn's way? I like flowers in a window.'

And Angelo scurried to arrange the window sill. Flynn's following eyes, from somewhere out of the steam, found Celeste's long back and strong legs – her broad, taut buttocks laboring under the weight of crocuses and anonymous greens, lilac branches and unopened buds.

There were very few girls who came to see the news on this Friday night, the last Friday of the school year, the last weekend before the final exams. Presumably the girls were studying, and those who weren't had chosen to go out and *really* not study (rather than compromise with the news). It had rained that afternoon, a rain you could smell, steaming off the sidewalks and leaving the streets nearly dry – only a few tepid puddles remained, and the evening air resembled the damp stuffiness of a laundromat. The heat was of that sensuous, gluttonous kind that people in Boston imagine is like the swamp-surrounded porches of a Southern estate, complete with a woman lolling nude in a hammock. Minna felt pleasantly tired; she sat by the window, looking out to the circular driveway in front of the dormitory. It was a private, gravel driveway with a high curb, and from the window it appeared to be carved, almost etched through the rows of elms and the green, green lawn. Minna saw Celeste, arms akimbo, sitting with her back against a tree. Her legs were extended straight in front of her so that her ankles stuck out over the curb of the driveway. It would have been an entirely unbecoming posture for almost any woman, but somehow Celeste lent to it a kind of magnificence in repose; a figure in semi-recline that seemed not exactly sluggish but rather wantonly indisposed to any motion. She was somewhat arrogantly dressed; a sleeveless, high-necked jersey, untucked and fallen outside one of those wrap-around skirts – the kind that always had a slit somewhere, and the slit on Celeste fell to the side of, and a little behind her hard, round thigh. She might have been a splendid Chinese madame, languishing alongside some still canal, waiting to hail a likely sampan as it wound its way through the eucalyptus trees.

The girls stayed after the news to hear the weather report, and to see the dapper little man in the weather station at Logan Airport painfully interpret his complex map. The girls' plans for the weekend obviously hinged on the good weather, and they were all there, Minna still at the window, Celeste still at the tree, when a motorcycle, the gas tank painted British Green, neatly cornered the right-angled entrance to the driveway, leaned cautiously into the gravel circle, and stopped (sliding just a little) in front of the dormitory. The motorcyclist was a young man, very tanned and very blond, with a remarkably babyish face. His shoulders were almost pointed and his head seemed too small for the rest of him; long, thin arms and legs, snugly fitted in a beige summer suit which sported a wild silk handkerchief in the breast pocket. He wore no tie, just a white shirt open at the throat. His passenger was Molly Cabot. Molly skipped lightly away from the cycle and the curb, then waited for the driver to step off his machine, which he did quite stiffly and slowly. He walked with Molly into the front lobby of the dormitory, walking in the manner of a stoically injured athlete. Minna turned, to see how the weather was progressing, and saw that all the girls were surrounding her at the window.

One of the girls said, 'So she *did* get a date with him!'

'We'll never hear the end of this,' another girl added.

Everyone sat or stooped rather gravely about the window, waiting for the cyclist to reappear. He wasn't long inside, and when he came out he looked all around him and fiddled with several screws on the motorcycle. His gestures seemed hurried and not really intended to fix anything; they were the gestures of one who was conscious of being watched. He rose up on the seat and came down heavily on the kick starter; the report which followed the first sucking sound was startling to those in the window. It even caught the attention of Celeste, who straightened up from her repose against the tree and sat a little further out on the curb. The motorcycle moved around the driveway in Celeste's direction and when it was a few feet past her the brake light flickered, the rear wheel slid gently sideways towards the curb, and the cyclist brought his right foot to the ground as the machine stopped. He then straightened up off the seat and walked the motorcycle backwards to where Celeste sat. One of the girls moved away from the window and shut off the television, then came quickly back to her position in the huddle. No-one could hear what the boy was saying because he kept the engine running. Celeste didn't seem to be saying anything. She just smiled, engaged looks of practiced scrutiny at the motorcycle and the boy. Then she got up, moved in front of the cycle, moved her hand once or twice in front of the headlamp, touched one of the instrument dials mounted on the handlebars, and stood back from the boy and his machine – giving what appeared from the window to be one last appraisal of everything that met her eyes. At that moment, or so it seemed to the window-watchers, Molly Cabot knocked once on the door of Minna's room, entered and said, 'Wow!' Everyone stood up and tried to be doing something, one girl made an awkward move to the television, but Molly came directly to the window and looked out to the driveway, asking, 'Has he gone?' She was in time to see Celeste offer her hand to the cyclist and deftly swing herself up behind him – executed with surprising agility for her long weight. The skirt was a slight problem, she had to twist it so that the slit was

115

directly behind her. Then she gripped the seat and the driver with her strong legs, rolled her long arms completely around him – her head was a full two inches higher than his, her back and her shoulders seemed broader, stronger than his. The cyclist shifted all his weight to his left leg, held the motorcycle up with some difficulty, and with his right foot shifted the machine into gear. They pulled away slowly, weaving slightly to the end of the driveway; then, once free of the gravel, and with a minimum of fish-tailing from the rear wheel, the cycle lurched into the traffic on the broad street. From the window they were able to follow the sound through the first three gears; then the machine and its riders either stayed in that gear or were lost to the window-watchers and listeners in the random blaring of horns and the other sounds of traffic in the night.

'That bastard,' Molly Cabot said, coolly, analytically – and from the faces of the other girls, expectedly.

'Maybe he's just taken her for a ride around the block,' someone said, not too convincingly, not even too hopefully.

'Sure,' Molly said, and she turned from the window and walked directly out of the room.

All the girls went back to the window. They sat for another twenty minutes, just looking into the night, and finally Minna said, 'It's surely time for the movie. Will anyone stay and see it with me?' It was suddenly a night when something extraordinary was called for, Minna thought, and so she considered the extravagance of asking all of them to stay for the movie. If Mrs Elwood came, as she might, she would not be pleased about it, would speak to Minna about it – after the girls were gone.

'Why not?' someone said.

The movie, as if things weren't cruel enough, was an old musical. The girls commented harshly on each new scene and song. During the commercials the girls went and sat by the window, and whenever there was a likely roar in the street they ran over, regardless of what new horror in song the movie then explored. When the movie was over the girls were unwilling to leave (some of them had rooms that didn't face the driveway), and they appeared bitterly resolved to a night-long vigil. Minna asked politely, shyly, if she might go to bed, and the girls straggled into the corridor, aimlessly bitching. They didn't seem angry at Celeste, or angry because they felt badly for Molly; on the contrary, it struck Minna that they were almost glad about it, and certainly excited. Their anger came from a feeling that they had been deeply cheated out of witnessing the climax to the show. They'll be up all night, Minna thought. How awful.

But Minna waited up herself. She occasionally dozed at the window, waking every time with a start – ashamed at the thought that someone might see her there, watching. It was after three when she went to bed, and she didn't sleep well. She was too tired to get up at every sound, but listened intently to them all. Finally she woke to a sound which was unmistakably the motorcycle, or at least *some* motorcycle. It was stopped at the beginning of the driveway, she could tell, still out on the street, the engine still running. It growled warily out there, making funny, laboring sounds. Then she heard it pull away, heard it pass through three gears again, and lost it as all of them had lost it before, many blocks or even miles away. She listened for the driveway itself now, for the little crunching sounds it makes while supporting feet. She heard the little pops

117

and snaps of the stones, the grating sound of feet and stones on the cement steps. She heard the screen door open, the main door open (she had thought, horribly, intriguingly, that it might have been locked), and then she heard, sometime later, the door at the end of the corridor. It was light in her room and she saw that it was nearly five o'clock. Angelo and Flynn would be in the kitchen soon, perhaps they were already there. Then she heard other doors open along the corridor, and the hurried, bare feet of the girls padding from room to room. She heard whispering and then she fell asleep.

Saturday morning it rained. A fine, inadequate kind of summer rain that did nothing but fog the windows and leave tiny beads of sweat on everyone's upper lip. It might just as well have been sunny and dazzling for all the difference it made on the temperature, and on Flynn's disposition. Flynn remarked, shortly before lunch, that there hadn't been so few people to breakfast since the flu epidemic in December. It always irritated him to prepare a lot of food and have no-one there to eat it. Also, he was bothered by the luncheon menu, angry that they were still serving soup when it was so damn hot (and no-one did anything but spill it anyway). Despite the weather, there were a lot of boys and parents in the dining hall. Minna always thought this odd, that everyone spent a year talking about the final exams, and that the weekend before the exams was invariably most festive.

Minna watched Celeste rather carefully that morning, wishing she could say something, although she couldn't think of what on earth she even wanted to say. It hadn't, of course, been wrong of Celeste, but Minna had to confess that Celeste just hadn't *looked* very nice. It was only sad because everyone had to *see* it, had to be hurt or angry because of it. And there wasn't much you could say about that. A peculiar uneasiness passed over Minna – some warm remembrance of a pervasive scent, fecund and coffee-rich, which quickly evanesced.

There was lunch to get ready. Most of the girls had filled the dining hall before the soup was served on every table. Angelo looked sadly at the drooping flowers on the many window sills, and received angry commands from Flynn that he finish serving the soup. Celeste worked steadily, carrying trays of potato salad, tureens of soup; every time she returned to the kitchen from the dining hall she took one luxurious pull on her cigarette, left dangling over the counter during her exits. Minna neatly arranged the lettuce in pretty patterns around the rim of the salad trays, being careful to hide the wilted and brown parts under the potatoes.

Celeste was taking what had to be the last drag on her cigarette when Molly Cabot swung open the aluminum door to the kitchen; she stepped inside, biting her lips, and allowed the door to swing closed behind her. Angelo, with a handful of flowers, turned to see who'd come in. Flynn stared indifferently. And Minna felt a tremendous weight on her diaphragm, pushing in or pushing out – it was hard to tell where the force was coming from. Molly Cabot, unsteady and small, stepped a little forward and away from the door. She squinted painfully at Celeste, in what might have been an attempt to intimidate the long, calm woman.

'You bitch, you whore!' Molly shouted. A voice as shrill and delicate as a coffee spoon striking a saucer. 'You *really* dirty whore!'

119

And Celeste just looked, smiling gently – an inquiring, still puzzled face which invited Molly to please continue.

Molly gained a certain composure, a practiced restraint of the kind suggested in Beginning Speech Class, and said, 'I will not stoop so low as to compete on *your* level!' It was not haughty, it was still the spoon on the saucer.

Minna said, 'Molly, dear. Don't.' And Molly, without taking her eyes from Celeste, stepped gingerly backwards, feeling for the door with her hand, and when her weight rested against the door she leaned back and swung with it – revolved out of the kitchen. The door swung back, bringing no new horrors in its path, swung twice before it squeaked and closed. Minna looked apologetically at Celeste. 'Celeste, dear,' she began, but Celeste turned to her with the same penetrating calm, the same inquiring face she had turned to Molly.

'It's all right, Minna,' she said, soothingly, as if she spoke to a child.

Minna shook her head and looked away; it seemed she would cry at any second. Then Flynn shook and clamored against the aluminum shelves. 'Christ!' he hollered. 'What's going on?'

There was a long moment when no-one spoke, and then there was Angelo; with a curiously studied fury that never could have been his own, but something mimicked from countless bad movies and college plays, he stepped awkwardly to the middle of the kitchen, throwing himself off balance as he flung his wilted flowers to the floor. 'Who does she think she is?' he demanded. 'Who does she think she's talking to? Who *is* she?'

'She's just a girl who thinks I stole her boy,' Celeste said. 'We went out for a ride last night, after he brought her back here.'

'But she can't say that!' Angelo cried, and Minna saw that the consistently pale face of Angelo was deeply flushed.

'I got a daughter her age,' Flynn said. 'I'd wash her damn mouth out with soap if she ever pulled any of that stuff.'

'Oh, that's really good, Flynn,' Celeste snapped, 'that's really good, coming from you! Why don't you just shut up?'

But Angelo, they should have known, had at last encountered the dark illogical fate which any one of them might have envisioned for him. He made some quick, secretive movement with his hands and walked to the aluminum door – like one who'd seen a specter of his potential self, beckon and bid him follow. He was gone before anyone could say anything, even before anyone could move, leaving the kitchen in ghoulish silence.

Then Flynn said, 'He took the lye soap out of the sink. He took it with him!' And Celeste moved more quickly than Flynn and Minna, moved in front of them, out through the swinging door.

The dining hall was very crowded, but very quiet. The occasional tinkle of ice cubes in the tea, the nervous creakings of chairs. Mrs Elwood sat at the Head Table, surrounded by well-dressed parents and children with napkins tucked into their collars. Minna looked helplessly at Mrs Elwood, whose chin was twitching in random little spasms. Angelo stood in the aisle between two rows of tables at the far end of the dining hall, the yellow-green bar of lye soap in his right hand – held as if it were extremely heavy or dangerous, held like a shot-put or a grenade. He stood like Odysseus, come home to Penelope, come home to throw the rabble of suitors out of his house to hack and behead them all – come fiercely to do great violence. Molly Cabot peered into her soup, prodigiously counting the noodles or rice. Angelo leaned across the table until his nose was almost in her hair.

'You got to apologize to Miss Celeste. Girl,' he said softly, 'you got to get up and do it right now.'

Molly didn't look up from her soup. She said, 'No, Angelo.' And then, very quietly, she added, 'You go back to the kitchen. Right now.'

Angelo put his hand on the edge of Molly's soup dish, palm up, and he let the bar of lye soap slide into her soup.

'Right now,' Angelo softly commanded. 'You apologize or I'll wash your mouth out good.'

Molly pushed her chair back from the table and began to stand up, but Angelo caught her by the shoulders, pulled her across the table to him, and began to force her head down, down to the soup dish. The girl sitting next to Molly screamed – one shrill and aimless scream – and Angelo got his hand on the back of Molly's neck and shoved her face into the soup. He dunked her swiftly, just once, and then he caught her by one shoulder and pulled her to him, his right hand groping for the soap. There was a boy sitting across the aisle from Molly's table. He jumped up and shouted, 'Hey!' But Celeste was the first to get to Angelo; she seized him around the waist and picked him off the floor, loosened his grip on Molly, and then tried to shift him over her hip, tried to carry him down the aisle to the kitchen. But Angelo wriggled free of her, wriggled into hairy Flynn. Flynn grabbed Angelo in a bear hug and everyone heard Angelo grunt. Flynn just turned and walked Angelo toward the kitchen, bending the thin body to a sharp curve at the spine; Celeste ran in front of them, got to the door first and held it open. Angelo kicked and clawed, snapping his head around to try and see where Molly had gone. 'You whore!' Angelo screamed, his breath pinched out of him in thin soprano. And then they passed through the great door – Angelo peering madly over the shoulders of Flynn – Celeste hurrying after them, the door swinging heavily closed.

Minna caught one glimpse of Molly Cabot, leaving the dining hall with a napkin over her face, her blouse spattered with soup and clinging to her bird-like chest. Her scalded, offended, demure breasts seemed to point the way of her determined exit. Then Mrs Elwood took Minna by the arm and whispered, confidingly, 'I must know what this is about. Whatever possessed him? He must leave at once. At once!'

In the kitchen Angelo sat in grand disorder on the floor, leaning against an aluminum cabinet. Flynn roughly dabbed at Angelo's mouth with a wet towel; Angelo was bleeding from his mouth, and he slumped, bespattered with soup, bleeding slowly down his chin. He moaned a high, complaining moan – the whine of an abandoned dog – and his eyes were closed.

'What did you do to him?' Celeste asked Flynn.

'He must have bit his tongue,' Flynn mumbled.

'I did, I did,' Angelo said, his voice muted by the towel which Flynn squeezed against his mouth.

'Christ, what a stupid Wop,' Flynn grumbled.

123

Celeste took the towel from Flynn and shoved him away from Angelo. 'Let me do that,' she said. 'You'll rub his whole face off.'

'I should have hit her,' Angelo blurted. 'I should have just hit her a good one.'

'Christ, listen to him!' Flynn shouted.

'Shut up, Flynn,' Celeste said.

And Minna, silent all this time, moused in a corner of the kitchen. She said, 'He'll have to leave. Mrs Elwood said he'll have to leave at once.'

'Christ, what'll he do?' Flynn asked. 'Where in Hell can he go?'

'Don't worry about me,' Angelo said. He blinked his eyes and smiled at Celeste. She knelt in front of him, made him open his mouth so that she could see his tongue; she had a clean handkerchief in the pocket of her dress and she gently touched his tongue with it, gently closed his mouth, took his hand and made him hold the wet towel to his lips. Angelo shut his eyes again, leaned forward, his head falling on Celeste's shoulder. Celeste settled back on her ankles, wrapped one great arm around Angelo and slowly rocked him, forward and backward, until he made himself into a little ball on her breast – his curious moan began again, only now it was more like someone making up a song.

'I'll lock the door,' Flynn said, 'so's no-one can come in.'

Minna watched, a dull ache in her throat, the prelude to great weeping and sorrow; and arising with the ache was a coldness in her hands and feet. This was hate – oddly enough, she thought – hate for Angelo's possessor, for Celeste, his captor, who now held him as if he were a wild, trapped rabbit. She calmed him, she would tame him; Angelo, dutifully, was her pet and her child, her charge – possessed by this vast, sensuous body, which now and forever would be his magnificent unachievable goal. And he wouldn't even be aware of what it was that held him to her.

'Angelo,' Celeste said softly, 'my brother-in-law has an inn, in Maine. It's very nice there, on the ocean, and there would be work for you – a free place to stay. In the winter it's quiet, just clean snow to be shoveled and things to be fixed. In the summer the tourists come to swim and sail; there's boats and beaches, and you'd like my family.'

'No,' Minna said. 'It's too far. How could he get there?'

'I'll take him myself,' Celeste told her. 'I'll drive him there tonight. I'd only miss one day, just tomorrow.'

'He's never been out of Boston,' Minna said. 'He wouldn't like it.'

'Of course he'd like it!' Flynn shouted. 'It'll be perfect.'

'Celeste?' Angelo asked. 'Will you be there?'

'On weekends, in the summer,' she said. 'And all my vacations.'

'What's it called?' Angelo asked her. He sat up, back against the counter cabinet, and he touched her hair with his hand. His wondering, adoring eyes passed over her thick, black hair, her strong-boned face and wide mouth.

'It's called Heron's Neck,' Celeste told him. 'Everybody's very friendly. You'd get to know them all, right away.'

'I'll bet you'd like it just fine, Angelo,' Flynn said.

'We'll go tonight,' Celeste prompted. 'We'll go as soon as we put your things in my car.'

'You can't do it,' Minna said. 'You can't take him there.'

'She'll only miss one day!' Flynn shouted. 'Christ, Minna, what's one day?'

Minna passed her hand over her face, the powder wet and clotted at the corners of her eyes. She looked at Celeste.

'You can't have the day off,' Minna told her. 'It's a busy time of year.'

'Christ!' Flynn hollered. 'Speak to Mrs Elwood about it!'

'I'm in charge of this kitchen!' Minna cried. 'I saw to getting her hired, and I'll see to this.' Flynn evaded Minna's eyes, and it was very quiet in the kitchen.

'What if I just left with Angelo tonight?' Celeste asked.

'Then you just leave for good,' Minna said.

'Put Angelo on a bus!' Flynn bellowed; great purple globes, welt-like, stood out on his cheeks.

'I don't want to go there alone!' Angelo cried. 'I don't know anybody,' he added meekly.

It was quiet again, and this time Flynn evaded Celeste's eyes. Celeste looked down at her knees, then she touched Angelo's damp head.

'I'll take you right now,' Celeste told him slowly.

'We'll be there together,' Angelo said, rapidly nodding his head. 'You can show me around.'

'It'll be nicer that way,' Celeste told him. 'We'll just do that.'

'I should say goodbye to Mrs Elwood,' Angelo said.

'Why don't we just send her a postcard when we get there,' Celeste suggested.

'Yeah,' Angelo said. 'And we can send one to Flynn

126

and to Minna. What kind of postcard do you want, Flynn?'

'Maybe one of the water and cliffs,' he answered gently.

'Cliffs, huh?' Angelo asked Celeste.

'Sure,' she said.

'What kind do you want, Minna?' Angelo asked, but she had turned away from them. She was stooping to pick up the flowers from the floor.

'Anything you'd like to send,' she told him.

'Then let's get ready,' Celeste said.

'Do you want to go out the other door?' Flynn asked. 'To get some air.' He opened the door which led to the campus yard. It had stopped raining. The grass was shiny and smelled very lush.

When they were gone, when Flynn had shut the door behind them, Minna said, 'Well, it's going to be busy with just the two of us, but I guess we'll get on.'

'Sure we'll get on,' Flynn told her. Then he added, 'I think that was a pretty stinking thing to do.'

'I *am* sorry, Flynn,' she said – a thin, breaking voice – and then she saw the tureens of soup, the trays of potato salad. God, she thought, have they been waiting out there all this time? But when she peeked into the dining hall, gingerly leaning on the door, she saw that everyone was gone. Mrs Elwood must have shooed them all away.

'There's no-one out there,' she told Flynn.

'Just look at all this food,' he said.

Before the news, before the movie. Minna sits in her room, waiting for it to be finally dark. A soft, gray light falls over the driveway and over the elms, and

127

Minna listens for sounds from Celeste's room – she watches for Celeste's car in the driveway. They must have gone by now, she thinks. They probably loaded the car somewhere else; Celeste would think of that. It is dusky in Minna's room; the faint light of early evening touches what few bright articles are placed on Minna's desk and bedside table, on the chest of drawers and television, on the coffee table. Most striking are the uneaten, unopened cans of foreign food. The hors d'oeuvre fork throws a dull reflection of the evening light back to Minna at the window. Poor Molly, Minna thinks— How awful that she has to go on *being* here, in front of everyone. And suddenly she feels the same sympathy for herself. It is a more ephemeral pity, though, and she soon feels thankful that school is so nearly over.

The street lights go on, whole rows of them lining the campus, giving the same luster to the elms and lawn that Minna noticed a night ago – a Chinese landscape, with canal, missing only Celeste. Minna moves from the window, turns on her desk lamp, mechanically hunts for a book. Then she sits deeply in the plush of her leather chair. She just sits, listening for nothing now, not reading, not even thinking. The toys of her weary mind seem lost.

A moth catches her eye. It has come from somewhere, somewhere safe, come to flutter wildly about the single light in the room. What on earth can it be that lures a moth out of the safety of darkness and into the peril of light? Its wings flap excitedly, it beats against the hot bulb of the lamp – it surely must scorch itself. Clumsily, carelessly, it bangs into things in an aimless frenzy. Minna thinks for a moment of getting up and turning off the light, but she doesn't feel like sitting in the dark – she doesn't feel like finding a newspaper to swat the moth. She sits, it grows darker, the buzz of the moth becomes soothing and pleasant. Minna dozes peacefully, briefly.

She wakes, startled, and thinks she is not awake – only dreaming. Then she sees the persistent moth and she knows she is really awake. It is completely dark outside now and she hears the familiar, restless growl of a motorcycle. She gets up from her chair and from the window she sees it, the same one, British Green. The cycle waits at the beginning of the driveway. Minna thinks, if he is coming for Molly he'll come into the dormitory. The cyclist glances around him, turns the throttle up and down, looks at his watch, jounces lightly on the seat. He has come for Celeste, Minna knows, and she watches him, aware that other windows around her are open, other eyes watching him. No-one comes out of the dormitory; Minna hears whispers pass from window screen to window screen, like a bird looking for a place to get in or out. The motorcyclist turns the throttle up again, holds the throttle there a moment, then lets the engine fall to its wary idle. Nothing happens, the cyclist jounces more heavily on the seat, looks again at his watch. Minna wonders, Do the girls know that Celeste is gone? Of course, the girls know everything; some of them probably knew that the motorcyclist would be back tonight, and not for Molly. But the cyclist is impatient now – sensing, perhaps, that Celeste isn't coming. Minna wishes she could see his face, but it is too dark. Only the pale blond hair flashes at her window, the lustrous green gas tank of the motorcycle shimmers like water; and then the throttle turns up again, the rear wheel skids sideways in the gravel, squeaks on the street. The whispering window screens are now silent, listening for the first three gears. Each gear seems to reach a little further than the night before.

Now Minna is alone with the moth. She wonders whether the girls will come for the news, wonders what time it is. And if the girls come, will Molly come with them? Oh, Minna hopes not, at least not tonight. The moth soothes her again, she dozes or half-dozes to the drone. She has a final, alarming thought before she falls to a deeper sleep. What will she ever say to Mrs Elwood? But the moth manages to calm even this. The happy, smudge-mouthed faces of her brother's children flood Minna's tiny room, and Angelo is somewhere among them. The motorcycle comes by once more, stops, snarls, goes madly on, ushered away to its dark journey by the titters at the window screens. But Minna doesn't hear it this time. She sleeps – lulled by the whirring, furry music of the moth.

# BRENNBAR'S RANT

My husband, Ernst Brennbar, worked steadily on his second cigar and his third cognac. A slow, rising heat flushed his cheeks. His tongue felt lazy and overweight. He knew that if he didn't try to speak soon, his mouth would loll open and he'd belch – or worse. A bear of guilt shifted in his stomach and he remembered the bottle of '64 Brauneberger Juffer Spätlese that had accompanied his ample portion of *truite Metternich.* His red ears throbbed a total recall of the '61 Pommard Rugiens that had drowned his *boeuf Crespi.*

Brennbar looked across the wasted dinner table at me, but I was lost in a conversation about minority groups. The man speaking to me appeared to be a member of one. For some reason, the waiter was included – perhaps as a gesture meant to absolve class distinctions. Perhaps because the man who spoke with me and the waiter were from the same minority group.

'You wouldn't know anything about it,' the man told me, but I'd been watching my blotching husband; I hadn't been paying attention.

'Well,' I said defensively, 'I can certainly imagine what it must have been like.'

'Imagine!' the man shouted. He tugged the waiter's sleeve for support. 'This was the real thing. No amount of *imagining* could ever make you feel it like we did. We had to live with it every day!' The waiter guessed he should agree.

Another woman, sitting next to Brennbar, suddenly said, 'That's no different from what women have always had to face – what we still have to face today.'

'Yes,' I said quickly, turning on the man. 'For example, you're bullying me right now.'

'Look, there's no persecution like religious persecution,' the man said, yanking the waiter's arm for accent.

'You might ask a black,' I said.

'Or any woman,' said the woman next to Brennbar. 'You talk as if you had a monopoly on discrimination.'

'You're all full of shit,' said Brennbar, slowly uncoiling his lounging tongue. The others stopped talking and looked at my husband as if he were a burn hole developing in a costly rug.

'Darling,' I said, 'we're talking about minority groups.'

'As if that counts me out?' Brennbar asked. He made me disappear in a roil of cigar smoke. But the woman next to him seemed to feel provoked by this; she responded recklessly.

'I don't see that you're black,' she said, 'or a woman or a Jew. You're not even Irish or Italian or something like that, are you? I mean – *Brennbar* – what's that? German?'

'*Oui*,' said the waiter. 'That's German, I know it.'

And the man whose pleasure had been to abuse me said, 'Oh, that's a fine minority group.' The others

– but not I – laughed. I was familiar with my husband's signals for the control he gradually lost on polite conversation; blowing cigar smoke in my face was a fairly advanced phase.

'My husband is from the Midwest,' I said cautiously.

'Oh, you poor man,' said the woman next to Brennbar. Her hand lay with facetious sympathy on Brennbar's shoulder.

'How appalling: the Midwest,' someone far down the table muttered.

And the man who held the waiter's sleeve with the importance he might lavish on a mine detector said, 'Now, there's a minority group!' Laughter embraced the table while I observed my husband's journey through one more lost control he held on polite conversation: the stiff smile accompanied by the studied tossing off of his third cognac and the oversteady pouring of his fourth.

I was so full I felt I'd temporarily lost my cleavage, but I said, 'I'd like dessert. Would anyone else have anything else?' I asked, watching the studied tossing off of my husband's fourth cognac and the fantastically deliberate pouring of his fifth.

The waiter remembered his job; he fled to fetch the menu. And the man who had sought in the waiter an ethnic kinship boldly faced Brennbar and said with unctuous condescension, 'I was merely trying to establish that religious discrimination – at least historically – is of a more subtle and pervasive kind than those forms of discrimination we have all jumped on the band wagon about lately, with our cries of racist, sexist—'

Brennbar belched: a sharp shot like a brass bedpost ball flung at random into the kitchenware. I was

135

familiar with this phase, too; I knew now that the dessert would come too late and that my husband scarcely needed to pause before he would launch forth.

Brennbar began: 'The first form of discrimination I encountered while growing up is so subtle and pervasive that even to this day no group has been able to organize to protest it, no politician has dared mention it, no civil-liberty case has been taken to the courts. In no major, nor in any minor, city is there even a suitable ghetto where these sufferers can support one another. Discrimination against them is so total that they even discriminate against one another; they are ashamed to be what they are, they are ashamed of it when they're alone – and all the more ashamed to be seen together.'

'Listen,' said the woman next to Brennbar, 'if you're talking about homosexuality, what you're saying is no longer the case—'

'I'm talking about pimples,' Brennbar said. 'Acne,' he added, with a meaningful and hurting glance about the table. 'Zits,' Brennbar said. The others, those who dared, stared into my husband's deeply cratered face as if they were peeking into a disaster ward in a foreign hospital. Alongside that terrible evidence, the fact that we were ordering dessert *after* brandy and cigars was of little consequence. 'You all knew people with pimples,' Brennbar accused them. 'And pimples disgusted you, didn't they?' The diners all looked away from him, but their memory of his pockmarks must have been severe. Those indentations, those pits, appeared to have been made by stones. My God, he was lovely.

Nearby, but coming no nearer, the waiter hovered and held back the dessert menus from this queer party as if he feared the menus could be consumed by our silence.

'Do you think it was easy to go into a drugstore?' Brennbar asked. 'A whole cosmetic counter devoted to reminding you, the saleslady grinning at your zits and saying loudly, "What can I do for you?" As if she didn't know. Even your own parents were ashamed of you! Subtle indications that your pillowcase was not washed with the rest of the laundry, and at breakfast your mother would say to you, "Dear, you know, don't you, that the *blue* washcloth is yours? " Then watch your sister's face pale; she excuses herself from the table and rushes to rewash. Talk about myths involved with discrimination! God, you'd think pimples were more communicative than clap! Some kid after gym class asks if someone has a comb; you offer him yours, you see his mind melt – praying for an alternative, imagining his precious scalp alive with your zits. It was a common fable: If you saw a pimple, you assumed dirt. People who produce pus never wash.

'I swear on my sister's sweet ass,' Brennbar said (he has no sister), 'I washed my entire body three times a day. One day I washed my face eleven times. Every morning I went to the mirror to read the news. Like a body count in a war. Maybe the acne plaster killed two overnight, but four more have arrived. You learn to expect the greatest humiliation at the worst time: The morning of the night you achieved that blind date, there's a new one pulling your lips askew. Then one day, out of misguided pity or a vast and unfathomable cruelty, those few people who pass for your friends secure you a date with *another* pimple freak! Mortified, you both wait for it to end. Did they expect we would exchange remedies or count our permanent scars?

'Zitism!' Brennbar yelled. 'That's what it is, zitism! And you're *zitists,* all of you, I'm sure of it,' he muttered. 'You couldn't begin to understand how awful . . .' His cigar was out; apparently shaken, he fumbled to relight it.

'No,' said the man next to me. 'I mean, yes . . . I can understand how terrible that must have been for you, really.'

'It's nothing like your problem,' Brennbar said morosely.

'No, well, yes – I mean, really, it *is* sort of what I mean,' the man groped. 'I can truly imagine how awful—'

'*Imagine?*' I said, my face alert, my mouth turning toward my best smile. 'But what about what you said to me? You can't possibly *feel* it like he did. He had to *live* with it every day.' I smiled at my husband. 'Those were real pimples,' I told my former attacker. 'They're not to be imagined.' Then I leaned across the table and touched Brennbar's hand affectionately. 'Nice work, darling,' I said. 'You got him.'

'Thanks,' said Brennbar, totally relaxed. His cigar was relit; he passed the rim of his brandy snifter under his nose like a flower.

The woman next to Brennbar was unsure. She touched him gently, but urgently, and said to him, 'Oh, I see, you were kidding – sort of. Weren't you?' Brennbar consumed her in cigar smoke before she could read his eyes; I can always read his eyes.

'Well, not kidding, exactly – were you, darling?' I said. 'I think it was a metaphor,' I told the others, and they looked at Brennbar with all the more suspicion. 'It was a metaphor for growing up with intelligence in a stupid world. It meant that intelligence is so peculiar

– so rare – that those of us with any real brains are constantly being discriminated against by the masses of stupidity around us.' The entire table looked more pleased. Brennbar smoked; he could be an infuriating man.

'Of course,' I went on, 'people with intelligence really constitute one of the smallest minority groups. They have to endure the wallowing sheep-mindedness and flagrant idiocy of what's forever being *popular.* Popularity is probably the greatest insult to an intelligent person. Hence,' I said, with a gesture to Brennbar, who was resembling a still life, 'acne is a perfect metaphor for the feeling of being unpopular, which every intelligent person must suffer. Intelligence is unpopular, of course. Nobody likes an intelligent person. Intelligent people are not to be trusted. We suspect that their intelligence hides a kind of perversity. It's a little like thinking that people with pimples are unclean.'

'Well,' began the man next to me – he was warming up to the conversation, which he must have felt was returning to more comfortable ground. 'Of course, the notion of the intellectual constituting a kind of ethnic group – this is hardly new. America is predominantly anti-intellectual. Look at television. Professor types are all batty eccentrics with the sort of temperaments of grandmothers. All idealists are fanatics or saints, young Hitlers or young Christs. Children who read books wear glasses and secretly wish they could play baseball as well as the other kids. We prefer an armpit evaluation of a man. And we like his mind to be possessed by the kind of stubborn loyalty we admire in dogs. But I must say, Brennbar, to suggest that pimples are analogous to intellect—'

'Not intellect,' I said. 'Intelligence. There are as many stupid intellectuals as there are stupid baseball players. Intelligence simply means the perception of what is going on.' But Brennbar was cloaked in an enigma of cigar smoke and even the woman next to him could not see through to his point of view.

The man who had momentarily experienced the illusion of returning to more comfortable ground said, 'I would dispute with you, Mrs Brennbar, that there are as many stupid intellectuals as there are stupid baseball players.'

Brennbar released a warning belch: a long, tunneling and muffled signal like a trash can thrown down an elevator shaft while you were far away, in a shower on the 31st floor ('Who's there?' you'd call out to your empty apartment).

'Dessert?' said the waiter, distributing menus. He must have thought Brennbar had asked for one.

'I'll have the *pommes Normande en belle vue,*' said the faraway man who had found the Midwest appalling. His wife wanted the *pouding alsacien,* a cold dessert.

'I'd like the *charlotte Malakoff aux fraises,*' said the woman next to Brennbar.

I said I'd have the *mousseline au chocolat.*

*'Shit,'* said Brennbar. Whatever he'd meant as a metaphor, his ravaged face was no invention; we could all see that.

'I was just trying to help you, darling,' I said, in a shocking new tone.

'Smart bitch,' Brennbar said.

The man for whom comfortable ground was now a hazardous free fall away sat in this uneasy atmosphere of warring minority feelings and wished for

140

more intelligence than he had. 'I'll have the *clafouti aux pruneaux,'* he said sheepishly.

'You would,' said Brennbar. 'That's just what I figured you for.'

'I got him right, too, darling,' I said.

'Did you guess *her*?' Brennbar asked me, indicating the woman next to him.

'Oh, she was easy,' I said. 'I got everyone.'

'I was wrong on yours,' Brennbar told me. He seemed troubled. 'I was sure you'd try to split the savarin with someone.'

'Brennbar doesn't eat dessert,' I explained to the others. 'It's bad for his complexion.'

Brennbar sat more or less still, like a contained lava flow. I knew that in a very short time we would go home. I wanted, terribly, to be alone with him.

# OTHER PEOPLE'S
DREAMS

Fred had no recollection of having had a dreamlife until his wife left him. Then he remembered some vague nightmares from his childhood, and some specific, lustful dreams from what seemed to him to be the absurdly short period of time between his arrival at puberty and his marrying Gail (he had married young). The ten dreamless years he had been married were too tender wounds for him to probe them very deeply, but he knew that in that time Gail had dreamed like a demon – one adventure after another – and he'd woken each morning feeling baffled and dull, searching her alert, nervous face for evidence of her nighttime secrets. She never told him her dreams, only that she had them – and that she found it very peculiar that he didn't dream. 'Either you do dream, Fred,' Gail told him, 'and your dreams are so sick that you prefer to forget them, or you're really dead. People who don't dream at all are quite dead.'

In the last few years of their marriage, Fred found neither theory so farfetched.

After Gail-left, he felt 'quite dead.' Even his girl friend, who had been Gail's 'last straw,' couldn't revive him. He thought that everything that had happened to his marriage had been his own fault: Gail had appeared to be happy and faithful – until he'd created some mess and she'd been forced to 'pay him back'. Finally, after he had repeated himself too many times, she had given up on him. 'Old fall-in-love Fred,' she called him. He seemed to fall in love with someone almost once a year. Gail said: 'I could possibly tolerate it, Fred, if you just went off and got laid, but why do you have to get so stupidly involved?'

He didn't know. After Gail's leaving, his girl friend appeared so foolish, sexless and foul to him that he couldn't imagine what had inspired his last, alarming affair. Gail had abused him so much for this one that he was actually relieved when Gail was gone, but he missed the child – they had just one child in ten years – a nine-year-old boy named Nigel. They'd both felt their own names were so ordinary that they had stuck their poor son with this label. Nigel now lay in a considerable portion of Fred's fat heart like an arrested case of cancer. Fred could bear not seeing the boy (in fact, they hadn't gotten along together since Nigel was five), but he could not stand the thought of the boy hating him, and he was sure Nigel hated him – or, in time, would learn to. Gail had learned to.

Sometimes Fred thought that if he'd only had dreams of his own, he wouldn't have had to act out his terrible love affairs with someone almost once a year.

For weeks after the settlement he couldn't sleep in the bed they'd shared for ten years. Gail settled for cash and Nigel. Fred kept the house. He slept on the couch, bothered by restless nights of blurry discomfort – too disjointed for dreams. He thrashed on the couch, his groaning disturbed the dog (he had settled for the dog, too), and his mouth in the morning was the mouth of a hangover – though he hadn't been drinking. One night he imagined he was throwing up in a car; the passenger in the car was Mrs Beal, and she was beating him with her purse while he retched and spilled over the steering wheel. 'Get us home! Get us home!' Mrs Beal cried at him. Fred didn't know then, of course, that he was having Mr Beal's dream. Mr Beal had passed out on Fred and Gail's couch many times; he had no doubt had that terrible dream there and had left it behind for the next troubled sleeper.

Fred simply gave up on the couch and sought the slim, hard bed in Nigel's room – a child's captain's bed, with little drawers built under it for underwear and six-guns. The couch had given Fred a backache, but he was not ready to resume his life in the bed he'd shared with Gail.

The first night he slept in Nigel's bed he understood what strange ability he suddenly possessed – or, what a strange ability had suddenly possessed him. He had a nine-year-old's dream – Nigel's dream. It was not frightening to Fred, but Fred knew it must have been pure terror for Nigel. In a field Fred-as-Nigel was trapped by a large snake. The snake was immediately comic to Fred-as-Fred, because it was finned like a serpent and breathed fire. The snake struck repeatedly at Fred-as-Nigel's chest; he was so stunned he couldn't scream. Far across the field Fred saw Fred the way Nigel would have seen him. 'Dad!' Fred-as-Nigel whispered. But the real Fred was standing over a smoldering fire-pit; they had just had a barbecue, apparently. Fred was pissing into the pit

147

– a strong stream of urine rising around him – and he didn't hear his son crying.

In the morning Fred decided that the dreams of nine-year-olds were obvious and trite. He had no fear of further dreams when he sought his own bed that night; at least, while he slept with Gail, he had never had a dream in that bed – and although Gail had been a steady dreamer, Fred hadn't had any of *her* dreams in that bed before. But sleeping alone is different from sleeping with someone else.

He crept into the cold bed in the room reft of the curtains Gail had sewn. Of course he had one of Gail's dreams. He was looking in a floor-length mirror, but he was seeing Gail. She was naked, and for only a second he thought he was having a dream of his own – possibly missing her, an erotic memory, a desirous agonizing for her to return. But the Gail in the mirror was not a Gail he had ever seen. She was old, ugly, and seeing her nakedness was like seeing a laceration you wished someone would quickly close. She was sobbing, her hands soaring beside her like gulls – holding up this and that garment, each more of a violation to her color and her features than the last. The clothes piled up at her feet and she finally sagged down on them, hiding her face from herself; in the mirror, the bumped vertebrae along her backbone looked to him (to her) like some back-alley staircase they had once discovered on their honeymoon in Austria. In an onion-domed village, this alley was the only dirty, suspicious path they had found. And the staircase which crooked out of sight had struck them both as ominous; it was the only way out of the alley, unless they retraced their steps, and Gail had suddenly said, 'Let's go back.' He immediately agreed. But before they turned away, an old woman reeled round the topmost part of the staircase and, appearing to lose her balance, fell heavily down the stairs. She'd been carrying some things: carrots, a bag of gnarled potatoes and a live goose whose paddle-feet were hobbled together. The woman struck her face when she fell and lay with her eyes open and her black dress bunched above her knees. The carrots spread like a bouquet on her flat, still chest. The potatoes were everywhere. And the goose, still hobbled, gabbled and struggled to fly. Fred, without once touching the woman, went straight to the goose, although – excepting dogs and cats – he had never touched a live animal before. He tried to untie the leather thong which bound the goose's feet together, but he was clumsy and the goose hissed at him and pecked him fiercely, painfully, on the cheek. He dropped the bird and ran after Gail, who was running out of the alley – the way they had come.

Now in the mirror Gail had gone to sleep on the pile of her unloved clothes on the floor. That was the way Fred had found her – the night he came home from his first infidelity.

He woke up from her dream in the bed alone. He had understood, before, that she had hated him for his infidelity, but this was the first time he realized that his infidelity had made her hate herself.

Was there no place in his own house he could sleep without someone else's dream? Where was it possible to develop a dream of his own? There was another couch, in the TV room, but the dog – an old male Labrador – usually slept there. 'Bear?' he called. 'Here, Bear.' Nigel had named the dog 'Bear'. But then Fred remembered how often he had seen Bear in the fits of his own dreams – woofling in his sleep, his hackles curled, his webbed feet running in place, his pink hard-on slapping his belly – and he thought that surely he had not sunk so low as to submit to dreams of rabbit-chasing, fighting the neighborhood weimaraner, humping the Beals' sad bloodhound bitch. Of course, baby-sitters had slept on that couch, and might he not expect some savory dream of *theirs*? Was it worth risking one of Bear's dreams for some sweet impression of that lacy little Janey Hobbs?

Pondering dog hair and recalling many unattractive baby-sitters, Fred fell asleep in a chair – a dreamless chair; he was lucky. He was learning that his new-found miracle-ability was a gift that was as harrowing as it was exciting. It's frequently true that we have offered to us much of the insecurity of sleeping with strangers, and little of the pleasure.

When his father died, he spent a week with his mother. To Fred's horror, she slept on the couch and offered him the master bedroom with its vastly historical bed. Fred could sympathize with his mother's reluctance to sleep there, but the bed and its potential for epic dreaming terrified him. His parents had always lived in this house, had always – since he could remember – slept on that bed. Both his mother and father had been dancers – slim, graceful people even in their retirement. Fred could remember their morning exercises, slow and yoga-like movements on the sun-room rug, always to Mozart, Fred viewed their old bed with dread. What embarrassing dreams, and *whose,* would enmesh him there?

He could tell, with some relief, that it was his mother's dream. Like most people, Fred sought rules

150

in the chaos, and he thought he had found one: impossible to dream a dead person's dream. At least his mother was alive. But Fred had expected some elderly sentiment for his father, some fond remembrance which he imagined old people had; he was not prepared for the lustiness of his mother's dream. He saw his father gamboling in the shower, soapy in the underarms and soapy and erect below. This was not an especially young dream, either; his father was already old, the hair white on his chest, his breasts distended in that old man's way — like the pouches appearing around a young girl's nipples. Fred dreamed his mother's hot, wet affection for the goatishness he'd never seen in his father. Appalled at their inventive, agile, even acrobatic lovemaking, Fred woke with a sense of his own dull sexuality, his clumsy straightforwardness. It was Fred's first sex dream as a woman; he felt so stupid to be learning now — a man in his thirties, and from his *mother* — precisely how women liked to be touched. He had dreamed how his mother came. How she quite cheerfully *worked* at it.

Too embarrassed to look in her eyes in the morning, Fred felt ashamed that he had not bothered to imagine this of her — that he'd assumed too *little* of her, and too little of Gail. Fred was still condescending enough, in the way a son is to his mother, to assume that if his mother's appetite was so rich, his wife's would surely have been richer. That this was perhaps not the case didn't occur to him.

He was sadly aware that his mother could not make herself do the morning exercises alone, and in the week he stayed with her — an unlikely comfort he felt himself to be — she seemed to be growing stiffer, less athletic, even gaining weight. He wanted to offer to accompany her with the exercises; to insist that she continue her good physical habits, but he had seen her *other* physical habits and his inferiority had left him speechless.

He was also bewildered to find that his instincts as a voyeur were actually stronger than his instincts as a proper son. Though he knew he would suffer his mother's erotic memories, each night, he would not abandon the bed for what he thought to be the dreamless floor. Had he slept there he would have encountered at least one of his father's dreams from the occasional nights that his father had slept on the floor. He would have disproven his easy theory that dead persons' dreams don't transfer to the living. His mother's dreams were simply stronger than his father's, so her dreams dominated the bed. Fred could, for example, have discovered his father's real feelings for his Aunt Blanche on the floor. But we are not known for our ability to follow through on our unearned discoveries. We are top-of-the-water adventurers who limit our opinions of the icebergs to what we can see.

Fred was learning something about dreams, but there was more that he was missing. Why, for instance, did he usually dream *historical* dreams? – that is, dreams which are really memories, or exaggerated memories of real events in our past, or secondhand dreams. There are other kinds of dreams – dreams of things that haven't happened. Fred did not know much about those. He didn't even consider that the dreams he was having *could* be his own – that they were simply as close to him as he dared to approach.

He returned to his divorced home, no longer intrepid.

He was a man who'd glimpsed in himself a wound of terminal vulnerability. There are many unintentionally cruel talents that the world, indiscriminately, hands out to us. Whether we can use these gifts we never asked for is not the world's concern.

# THE PENSION
# GRILLPARZER

My father worked for the Austrian Tourist Bureau. It was my mother's idea that our family travel with him when he went on the road as a Tourist Bureau spy. My mother and brother and I would accompany him on his secretive missions to uncover the discourtesy, the dust, the badly cooked food, the shortcuts taken by Austria's restaurants and hotels and pensions. We were instructed to create difficulties whenever we could, never to order exactly what was on the menu, to imitate a foreigner's odd requests – the hours we would like to have our baths, the need for aspirin and directions to the zoo. We were instructed to be civilized but troublesome; and when the visit was over, we reported to my father in the car.

My mother would say, 'The hairdresser is always closed in the morning. But they make suitable recommendations outside. I guess it's all right, provided they don't claim to have a hairdresser actually *in* the hotel.'

'Well, they *do* claim it,' my father would say. He'd note this in a giant pad.

I was always the driver. I said, 'The car is parked off the street, but someone put fourteen kilometers on the gauge beween the time we handed it over to the doorman and picked it up at the hotel garage.'

'That is a matter to report directly to the management,' my father said, jotting it down.

'The toilet leaked,' I said.

'I couldn't open the door to the WC,' said my brother, Robo.

'Robo,' Mother said, 'you always have trouble with doors.'

'Was that supposed to be Class C?' I asked.

'I'm afraid not,' Father said. 'It is still listed as Class B.' We drove for a short while in silence; our most serious judgment concerned changing a hotel's or a pension's rating. We did not suggest reclassification frivolously.

'I think this calls for a letter to the management,' Mother suggested. 'Not too nice a letter, but not a really rough one. Just state the facts.'

'Yes, I rather liked him,' Father said. He always made a point of getting to meet the managers.

'Don't forget the business of them driving our car,' I said. 'That's really unforgivable.'

'And the eggs were bad,' said Robo; he was not yet ten and his judgments were not considered seriously.

We became a far harsher team of evaluators when my grandfather died and we inherited Grandmother – my mother's mother, who thereafter accompanied us on our travels. A regal dame, Johanna was accustomed to Class A travel, and my father's duties more frequently called for investigations of Class B and Class C lodgings. They were the places, the B and C hotels (and the pensions), that most interested the tourists. At restaurants we did a little better. People who couldn't afford the classy places to sleep were still interested in the best places to eat.

'I shall not have dubious food tested on me,' Johanna told us. 'This strange employment may give you all glee about having free vacations, but I can see there is a terrible price paid: the anxiety of not knowing what sort of quarters you'll have for the night. Americans may find it charming that we still have rooms without private baths and toilets, but I am an old woman and I'm not charmed by walking down a public corridor in search of cleanliness and my relievement. Anxiety is only half of it. Actual diseases are possible – and not only from food. If the bed is questionable, I promise I shan't put my head down. And the children are young and impressionable; you should think of the clientele in some of these lodgings and seriously ask yourselves about the influences.' My mother and father nodded; they said nothing. 'Slow down!' Grandmother said sharply to me. 'You're just a young boy who likes to show off.' I slowed down. 'Vienna,' Grandmother sighed. 'In Vienna I always stayed at the Ambassador.'

'Johanna, the Ambassador is not under investigation,' Father said.

'I should think not,' Johanna said. 'I suppose we're not even headed toward a Class A place?'

'Well, it's a B trip,' my father admitted. 'For the most part.'

'I trust,' Grandmother said, 'that you mean there is one A place en route?'

'No,' Father admitted. 'There is one C place.'

'It's okay,' Robo said. 'There are fights in Class C.'

'I should imagine so,' Johanna said.

'It's a Class C pension, very small,' Father said, as if the size of the place forgave it.

'And they're applying for a B,' said Mother.

'But there have been some complaints,' I added.

'I'm sure there have,' Johanna said.

'And animals,' I added. My mother gave me a look.

'Animals?' said Johanna.

'Animals,' I admitted.

'A *suspicion* of animals,' my mother corrected me.

'Yes, be fair,' Father said.

'Oh, wonderful!' Grandmother said. 'A suspicion of animals. Their hair on the rugs? Their terrible waste in the corners! Did you know that my asthma reacts, severely, to any room in which there has recently been a cat?'

'The complaint was not about cats,' I said. My mother elbowed me sharply.

'Dogs?' Johanna said. 'Rabid dogs! Biting you on the way to the bathroom.'

'No,' I said. 'Not dogs.'

'Bears!' Robo cried.

But my mother said, 'We don't know for sure about the bear, Robo.'

'This isn't serious,' Johanna said.

'Of course it's not serious!' Father said. 'How could there be bears in a pension?'

'There was a letter saying so,' I said. 'Of course, the Tourist Bureau assumed it was a crank complaint. But then there was another sighting – and a second letter claiming there had been a bear.'

My father used the rear-view mirror to scowl at me, but I thought that if we were all supposed to be in on the investigation, it would be wise to have Grandmother on her toes.

'It's probably not a real bear,' Robo said, with obvious disappointment.

'A man in a bear suit!' Johanna cried. 'What unheard-of perversion is *that*? A *beast* of a man sneaking about in disguise! Up to what? It's a man in a bear suit, I know it is,' she said. 'I want to go to that one *first*! If there's going to be a Class C experience on this trip, let's get it over with as soon as possible.'

'But we haven't got reservations for tonight,' Mother said.

'Yes, we might as well give them a chance to be at their best,' Father said. Although he never revealed to his victims that he worked for the Tourist Bureau, Father believed that reservations were simply a decent way of allowing the personnel to be as prepared as they could be.

'I'm sure we don't need to make a reservation in a place frequented by men who disguise themselves as animals,' Johanna said. 'I'm sure there is *always* a vacancy there. I'm sure the guests are regularly dying in their beds – of fright, or else of whatever unspeakable injury the madman in the foul bear suit does to them.'

'It's probably a *real* bear,' Robo said, hopefully – for in the turn the conversation was taking, Robo certainly saw that a real bear would be preferable to Grandmother's imagined ghoul. Robo had no fear, I think, of a real bear.

I drove us as inconspicuously as possible to the dark, dwarfed corner of Planken and Seilergasse. We were looking for the Class C pension that wanted to be a B.

'No place to park,' I said to Father, who was already making note of that in his pad.

I double-parked and we sat in the car and peered up at the Pension Grillparzer; it rose only four slender

161

stories between a pastry shop and a Tabak Trafik.

'See?' Father said. 'No bears.'

'No *men,* I hope,' said Grandmother.

'They come at night,' Robo said, looking cautiously up and down the street.

We went inside to meet the manager, a Herr Theobald, who instantly put Johanna on her guard. 'Three generations traveling together!' he cried. 'Like the old days,' he added, especially to Grandmother, 'before all these divorces and the young people wanting apartments by themselves. This is a *family* pension! I just wish you had made a reservation – so I could put you more closely together.'

'We're not accustomed to sleeping in the same room,' Grandmother told him.

'Of course not!' Theobald cried. 'I just meant that I wished your *rooms* could be closer together.' This worried Grandmother, clearly.

'How far apart must we be put?' she asked.

'Well, I've only two rooms left,' he said. 'And only one of them is large enough for the two boys to share with their parents.'

'And my room is how far from theirs?' Johanna asked coolly.

'You're right across from the WC!' Theobald told her, as if this were a plus.

But as we were shown to our rooms, Grandmother staying with Father – contemptuously to the rear of our procession – I heard her mutter, 'This is not how I conceived of my retirement. Across the hall from a WC, listening to all the visitors.'

'Not one of these rooms is the same,' Theobald told us. 'The furniture is all from my family.' We could believe it. The one large room Robo and I were to share with my parents was a half-sized museum of knickknacks, every dresser with a different style of knob. On the other hand, the sink had brass faucets and the headboard of the bed was carved. I could see my father balancing things up for future notation in the giant pad.

'You may do that later,' Johanna informed him. 'Where do *I* stay?'

As a family, we dutifully followed Theobald and my grandmother down the long, twining hall, my father counting the paces to the WC. The hall rug was thin, the color of a shadow. Along the walls were old photographs of speed-skating teams – on their feet the strange blades curled up at the tips like court jesters' shoes or the runners of ancient sleds.

Robo, running far ahead, announced his discovery of the WC.

Grandmother's room was full of china, polished wood, and the hint of mold. The drapes were damp. The bed had an unsettling ridge at its center, like fur risen on a dog's spine – it was almost as if a very slender body lay stretched beneath the bedspread.

Grandmother said nothing, and when Theobald reeled out of the room like a wounded man who's been told he'll live, Grandmother asked my father, 'On what basis can the Pension Grillparzer hope to get a B?'

'Quite decidedly C,' Father said.

'Born C and will die C,' I said.

'I would say, myself,' Grandmother told us, 'that it was E or F.'

In the dim tearoom a man without a tie sang a Hungarian song. 'It does not mean he's Hungarian,' Father reassured Johanna, but she was skeptical.

'I'd say the odds are not in his favor,' she suggested.

163

She would not have tea or coffee. Robo ate a little cake, which he claimed to like. My mother and I smoked a cigarette; she was trying to quit and I was trying to start. Therefore, we shared a cigarette between us – in fact, we'd promised never to smoke a whole one alone.

'He's a great guest,' Herr Theobald whispered to my father; he indicated the singer. 'He knows songs from all over.'

'From Hungary, at least,' Grandmother said, but she smiled.

A small man, clean-shaven but with that permanent gun-blue shadow of a beard on his lean face, spoke to my grandmother. He wore a clean white shirt (but yellow from age and laundering), suit pants, and an unmatching jacket.

'Pardon me?' said Grandmother.

'I said that I tell dreams,' the man informed her.

'You *tell* dreams,' Grandmother said. 'Meaning, you *have* them?'

'Have them and tell them,' he said mysteriously. The singer stopped singing.

'Any dream you want to know,' said the singer. 'He can tell it.'

'I'm quite sure I don't want to know any,' Grandmother said. She viewed with displeasure the ascot of dark hair bursting out at the open throat of the singer's shirt. She would not regard the man who 'told' dreams at all.

'I can see you are a lady,' the dream man told Grandmother. 'You don't respond to just every dream that comes along.'

'Certainly not,' said Grandmother. She shot my father one of her how-could-you-have-let-this-happen-to-me? looks.

'But I know one,' said the dream man; he shut his eyes. The singer slipped a chair forward and we suddenly realized he was sitting very close to us. Robo, though he was much too old for it, sat in Father's lap. 'In a great castle,' the dream man began, 'a woman lay beside her husband. She was wide awake, suddenly, in the middle of the night. She woke up without the slightest idea of what had awakened her, and she felt as alert as if she'd been up for hours. It was also clear to her, without a look, a word, or a touch, that her husband was wide awake too – and just as suddenly.'

'I hope this is suitable for the child to hear, ha ha,' Herr Theobald said, but no-one even looked at him. My grandmother folded her hands in her lap and stared at them – her knees together, her heels tucked under her straight-backed chair. My mother held my father's hand.

I sat next to the dream man, whose jacket smelled like a zoo. He said, 'The woman and her husband lay awake listening for sounds in the castle, which they were only renting and did not know intimately. They listened for sounds in the courtyard, which they never bothered to lock. The village people always took walks by the castle; the village children were allowed to swing on the great courtyard door. What had woken them?'

'Bears?' said Robo, but Father touched his fingertips to Robo's mouth.

'They heard horses,' said the dream man. Old Johanna, her eyes shut, her head inclined toward her lap, seemed to shudder in her stiff chair. 'They heard the breathing and stamping of horses who were trying to keep still,' the dream man said. 'The husband reached out and touched his wife. "Horses?" he said. The woman got out of bed and went to the

165

courtyard window. She would swear to this day that the courtyard was full of soldiers on horseback – but *what* soldiers they were! They wore *armor*! The visors on their helmets were closed and their murmuring voices were as tinny and difficult to hear as voices on a fading radio station. Their armor clanked as their horses shifted restlessly under them.

'There was an old dry bowl of a former fountain, there in the castle's courtyard, but the woman saw that the fountain was flowing; the water lapped over the worn curb and the horses were drinking it. The knights were wary, they would not dismount; they looked up at the castle's dark windows, as if they knew they were uninvited at this watering trough – this rest station on their way, somewhere.

'In the moonlight the woman saw their big shields glint. She crept back to bed and lay rigidly against her husband.

'"What is it?" he asked her.

'"Horses," she told him.

'"I thought so," he said. "They'll eat the flowers."

'"Who built this castle?" she asked him. It was a very old castle, they both knew that.

'"Charlemagne," he told her; he was going back to sleep.

'But the woman lay awake, listening to the water which now seemed to be running all through the castle, gurgling in every drain, as if the old fountain were drawing water from every available source. And there were the distorted voices of the whispering knights – *Charlemagne*'s soldiers speaking their dead language! To this woman, the soldiers' voices were as morbid as the eighth century and the people called Franks. The horses kept drinking.

166

'The woman lay awake a long time, waiting for the soldiers to leave; she had no fear of actual attack from them – she was sure they were on a journey and had only stopped to rest at a place they once knew. But for as long as the water ran she felt that she mustn't disturb the castle's stillness or its darkness. When she fell asleep, she thought Charlemagne's men were still there.

'In the morning her husband asked her, "Did you hear water running, too?" Yes, she had, of course. But the fountain was dry, of course, and out the window they could see that the flowers weren't eaten – and everyone knows horses eat flowers.

'"Look," said her husband; he went into the courtyard with her. "There are *no* hoofprints, there are no droppings. We must have *dreamed* we heard horses." She did not tell him that there were soldiers, too; or that, in her opinion, it was unlikely that two people would dream the same dream. She did not remind him that he was a heavy smoker who never smelled the soup simmering; the aroma of horses in the fresh air was too subtle for him.

'She saw the soldiers, or dreamed them, twice more while they stayed there, but her husband never again woke up with her. It was always sudden. Once she woke with the taste of metal on her tongue as if she'd touched some old, sour iron to her mouth – a sword, a chest plate, chain mail, a thigh guard. They were out there again, in colder weather. From the water in the fountain a dense fog shrouded them; the horses were snowy with frost. And there were not so many of them the next time – as if the winter or their skirmishes were reducing their numbers. The last time the horses looked gaunt to her, and the men looked more like unoccupied suits of armor balanced delicately in the saddles. The horses wore long masks of ice on their muzzles. Their breathing (or the men's breathing) was congested.

'Her husband,' said the dream man, 'would die of a respiratory infection. But the woman did not know it when she dreamed this dream.'

My grandmother looked up from her lap and slapped the dream man's beard-gray face. Robo stiffened in my father's lap; my mother caught her mother's hand. The singer shoved back his chair and jumped to his feet, frightened, or ready to fight someone, but the dream man simply bowed to Grandmother and left the gloomy tearoom. It was as if he'd made a contact with Johanna that was vital but gave neither of them any joy. My father wrote something in the giant pad.

'Well, wasn't *that* some story?' said Herr Theobald. 'Ha ha.' He rumpled Robo's hair – something Robo always hated.

'Herr Theobald,' my mother said, still holding Johanna's hand, *'my father died of a respiratory infection.'*

'Oh, dear shit,' said Herr Theobald. 'I'm sorry, *meine Frau,'* he told Grandmother, but old Johanna would not speak to him.

We took Grandmother out to eat in a Class A restaurant, but she hardly touched her food. 'That person was a gypsy,' she told us. 'A satanic being, and a Hungarian.'

'Please, Mother,' my mother said. 'He couldn't have known about Father.'

'He knew more than you know,' Grandmother snapped.

'The schnitzel is excellent,' Father said, writing in the pad. 'The Gumpoldskirchner is just right with it.'

'The Kalbsnieren are fine,' I said.

168

'The eggs are okay,' said Robo.

Grandmother said nothing until we returned to the Pension Grillparzer, where we noticed that the door to the WC was hung a foot or more off the floor, so that it resembled the bottom half of an American toilet-stall door or a saloon door in the Western movies. 'I'm certainly glad I used the WC at the restaurant,' Grandmother said. 'How revolting! I shall try to pass the night without exposing myself where every passerby can peer at my ankles!'

In our family room Father said, 'Didn't Johanna live in a castle? Once upon a time, I thought she and Grandpa rented some castle.'

'Yes, it was before I was born,' Mother said. 'They rented Schloss Katzelsdorf. I saw the photographs.'

'Well, *that's* why the Hungarian's dream upset her,' Father said.

'Someone is riding a bike in the hall,' Robo said. 'I saw a wheel go by – under our door.'

'Robo, go to sleep,' Mother said.

'It went "squeak squeak",' Robo said.

'Good night, boys,' said Father.

'If you can talk, we can talk,' I said.

'Then talk to each other,' Father said. 'I'm talking to your mother.'

'I want to go to sleep,' Mother said. 'I wish no-one would talk.'

We tried. Perhaps we slept. Then Robo whispered to me that he had to use the WC.

'You know where it is,' I said.

Robo went out the door, leaving it slightly open; I heard him walk down the corridor, brushing his hand along the wall. He was back very quickly.

'There's someone *in* the WC,' he said.

169

'Wait for them to finish,' I said.

'The light wasn't on,' Robo said, 'but I could still see under the door. Someone is in there, in the dark.'

'I prefer the dark myself,' I said.

But Robo insisted on telling me exactly what he'd seen. He said that under the door was a pair of *hands*.

'Hands?' I said.

'Yes, where the feet should have been,' Robo said; he claimed that there was a hand on either side of the toilet – instead of a foot.

'Get out of here, Robo!' I said.

'Please come see,' he begged. I went down the hall with him but there was no-one in the WC. 'They've gone,' he said.

'Walked off on their hands, no doubt,' I said. 'Go pee. I'll wait for you.'

He went into the WC and peed sadly in the dark. When we were almost back to our room together, a small dark man with the same kind of skin and clothes as the dream man who had angered Grandmother passed us in the hall. He winked at us, and smiled, I had to notice that he was walking on his hands.

'You see?' Robo whispered to me. We went into our room and shut the door.

'What is it?' Mother asked.

'A man walking on his hands,' I said.

'A man *peeing* on his hands,' Robo said.

'Class C,' Father murmured in his sleep; Father often dreamed that he was making notes in the giant pad.

'We'll talk about it in the morning,' Mother said.

'He was probably just an acrobat who was showing off for you, because you're a kid,' I told Robo.

'How did he know I was a kid when he was in the WC?' Robo asked me.

'Go to *sleep,'* Mother whispered.

Then we heard Grandmother scream down the hall.

Mother put on her pretty green dressing gown; Father put on his bathrobe and glasses. I pulled on a pair of pants, over my pajamas. Robo was in the hall first. We saw the light coming from under the WC door. Grandmother was screaming rhythmically in there.

'Here we are!' I called to her.

'Mother, what is it?' my mother asked.

We gathered in the broad slot of light. We could see Grandmother's mauve slippers and her porcelain-white ankles under the door. She stopped screaming. 'I heard whispers when I was in my bed,' she said.

'It was Robo and me,' I told her.

'Then, when everyone seemed to have gone, I came into the WC,' Johanna said. 'I left the light *off.* I was *very* quiet,' she told us. 'Then I saw and heard the wheel.'

'The *wheel*?' Father asked.

'A wheel went by the door a few times,' Grandmother said. 'It rolled by and came back and rolled by again.'

Father made his fingers roll like wheels alongside his head; he made a face at Mother. 'Somebody needs a new set of wheels,' he whispered, but Mother looked crossly at him.

'I turned on the light,' Grandmother said, 'and the wheel went away.'

'I told you there was a bike in the hall,' said Robo.

'Shut up, Robo,' Father said.

'No, it was not a bicycle,' Grandmother said. 'There was only one wheel.'

Father was making his hands go crazy beside his head. 'She's got a wheel or two *missing*,' he hissed at my mother, but she cuffed him and knocked his glasses askew on his face.

'Then someone came and looked *under* the door,' Grandmother said, 'and *that is* when I screamed.'

'Someone?' said Father.

'I saw his hands, a man's hands – there was hair on his knuckles,' Grandmother said. 'His hands were on the rug right outside the door. He must have been looking up at me.'

'No, Grandmother,' I said. 'I think he was just standing out here on his hands.'

'Don't be fresh,' my mother said.

'But we saw a man walking on his hands,' Robo said.

'You did *not*,' Father said.

'We *did*,' I said.

'We're going to wake everyone up,' Mother cautioned us.

The toilet flushed and Grandmother shuffled out the door with only a little of her former dignity intact. She was wearing a gown over a gown over a gown; her neck was very long and her face was creamed white. Grandmother looked like a troubled goose. 'He was evil and vile,' she said to us. 'He knew terrible magic.'

'The man who looked at you?' Mother asked.

'That man who told my *dream,*' Grandmother said. Now a tear made its way through her furrows of face cream. 'That was *my* dream,' she said, 'and he told everyone. It is unspeakable that he even *knew* it,' she hissed to us. '*My* dream – of Charlemagne's horses and soldiers – I am the only one who should know it. I had that dream before you were born,' she told Mother. 'And that vile evil magic man told my dream as if it were *news.*

'I never even told your father all there was to that dream. I was never sure that it *was* a dream. And now there are men on their hands, and their knuckles are hairy, and there are magic wheels. I want the boys to sleep with *me*.'

So that was how Robo and I came to share the large family room, far away from the WC, with Grandmother, who lay on my mother's and father's pillows with her creamed face shining like the face of a wet ghost. Robo lay awake watching her. I do not think Johanna slept very well; I imagine she was dreaming her dream of death again – reliving the last winter of Charlemagne's cold soldiers with their strange metal clothes covered with frost and their armor frozen shut.

When it was obvious that I had to go to the WC, Robo's round, bright eyes followed me to the door.

There was someone in the WC. There was no light shining from under the door, but there was a unicycle parked against the wall outside. Its rider sat in the dark WC; the toilet was flushing over and over again – like a child, the unicyclist was not giving the tank time to refill.

I went closer to the gap under the WC door, but the occupant was not standing on his or her hands. I saw what were clearly feet, in almost the expected position, but the feet did not touch the floor; their soles tilted up to me – dark, bruise-colored pads. They were *huge* feet attached to short, furry shins. They were a *bear*'s feet, only there were no claws. A bear's claws are not retractable, like a cat's; if a bear had claws, you would see them. Here, then, was an impostor in a bear suit, or a declawed bear. A domestic bear, perhaps. At least – by its presence in the WC – a *housebroken* bear. For by its smell I could tell it was no man in a bear suit; it was all bear. It was real bear.

I backed into the door of Grandmother's former room, behind which my father lurked, waiting for further disturbances. He snapped open the door and I fell inside, frightening us both. Mother sat up in bed and pulled the feather quilt over her head. 'Got him!' Father cried, dropping down on me. The floor trembled; the bear's unicycle slipped against the wall and fell into the door of the WC, out of which the bear suddenly shambled, stumbling over its unicycle and lunging for its balance. Worriedly, it stared across the hall, through the open door, at Father sitting on my chest. It picked up the unicycle in its front paws. '*Grauf?*' said the bear. Father slammed the door.

Down the hall we heard a woman call, 'Where are you, Duna?'

'*Harf!*' the bear said.

Father and I heard the woman come closer. She said, 'Oh, Duna, practicing again? Always practicing! But it's better in the daytime.' The bear said nothing. Father opened the door.

'Don't let anyone else in,' Mother said, still under the featherbed.

In the hall a pretty, aging woman stood beside the bear, who now balanced in place on its unicycle, one huge paw on the woman's shoulder. She wore a vivid red turban and a long wrap-around dress that resembled a curtain. Perched on her high bosom was a necklace strung with bear claws; her earrings touched the shoulder of her curtain-dress and her other, bare shoulder where my father and I stared at her fetching mole. 'Good evening,' she said to Father. 'I'm sorry if we've disturbed you. Duna is forbidden to practice at night – but he loves his work.'

174

The bear muttered, pedaling away from the woman. The bear had very good balance but he was careless; he brushed against the walls of the hall and touched the photographs of the speed-skating teams with his paws. The woman, bowing away from Father, went after the bear calling, 'Duna, Duna,' and straightening the photographs as she followed him down the hall.

'*Duna* is the Hungarian word for the Danube,' Father told me. 'That bear is named after our beloved *Donau*.' Sometimes it seemed to surprise my family that the Hungarians could love a river, too.

'Is the bear a *real* bear?' Mother asked – still under the featherbed – but I left Father to explain it all to her. I knew that in the morning Herr Theobald would have much to explain, and I would hear everything reviewed at that time.

I went across the hall to the WC. My task there was hurried by the bear's lingering odor, and by my suspicion of bear hair on everything; it was only my suspicion, though, for the bear had left everything quite tidy – or at least neat for a bear.

'I saw the bear,' I whispered to Robo, back in our room, but Robo had crept into Grandmother's bed and had fallen asleep beside her. Old Johanna was awake, however.

'I saw fewer and fewer soldiers,' she said. 'The last time they came there were only nine of them. Everyone looked so hungry; they must have eaten the extra horses. It was so cold. Of course I wanted to help them! But we weren't alive at the same time; how could I help them if I wasn't even born? Of course I knew they would die! But it took such a long time.

'The last time they came, the fountain was frozen.

175

They used their swords and their long pikes to break the ice into chunks. They built a fire and melted the ice in a pot. They took bones from their saddlebags – bones of all kinds – and threw them in the soup. It must have been a very thin broth because the bones had long ago been gnawed clean. I don't know what bones they were. Rabbits', I suppose, and maybe a deer or a wild boar. Maybe the extra horses. I do not choose to think,' said Grandmother, 'that they were the bones of the missing soldiers.'

'Go to sleep, Grandmother,' I said.

'Don't worry about the bear,' she said.

In the breakfast room of the Pension Grillparzer we confronted Herr Theobald with the menagerie of his other guests who had disrupted our evening. I knew that (as never before) my father was planning to reveal himself as a Tourist Bureau spy.

'Men walking about on their hands,' said Father.

'Men looking under the door of the WC,' said Grandmother.

'*That* man,' I said, and pointed to the small, sulking fellow at the corner table, seated for breakfast with his cohorts – the dream man and the Hungarian singer.

'He does it for a living,' Herr Theobald told us, and as if to demonstrate that this was so, the man who stood on his hands began to stand on his hands.

'Make him stop that,' Father said. 'We know he can do it.'

'But did you know that he can't do it any other way?' the dream man asked suddenly. 'Did you know that his legs were useless? He has no shinbones. It is *wonderful* that he can walk on his hands! Otherwise, he wouldn't walk at all.' The man, although it was clearly hard to do while standing on his hands, nodded his head.

'Please sit down,' Mother said.

'It is perfectly all right to be crippled,' Grandmother said, boldly. 'But you are evil,' she told the dream man. 'You know things you have no right to know. He knew my *dream,'* she told Herr Theobald, as if she were reporting a theft from her room.

'He is a *little* evil, I know,' Theobald admitted. 'But not usually! And he behaves better and better. He can't help what he knows.'

'I was just trying to straighten you out,' the dream man told Grandmother. 'I thought it would do you good. Your husband has been dead quite a while, after all, and it's about time you stopped making so much of that dream. You're not the only person who's had such a dream.'

'Stop it,' Grandmother said.

'Well, you ought to know,' said the dream man.

'No, be quiet, please,' Herr Theobald told him.

'I am from the Tourist Bureau,' Father announced, probably because he couldn't think of anything else to say.

'Oh my God shit!' Herr Theobald said.

'It's not Theobald's fault,' said the singer. 'It's *our* fault. He's nice to put up with us, though it costs him his reputation.'

'They married my sister,' Theobald told us. 'They are *family, you* see. What can I do?'

' "They" married your sister?' Mother said.

'Well, she married *me* first,' said the dream man.

'And then she heard *me* sing!' the singer said.

'She's never been married to the *other* one,' Theobald said, and everyone looked apologetically toward the man who could only walk on his hands.

Theobald said, 'They were once a circus act, but politics got them in trouble.'

'We were the best in Hungary,' said the singer. 'You ever hear of the Circus Szolnok?'

'No, I'm afraid not,' Father said, seriously.

'We played in Miskolc, in Szeged, in Debrecen,' said the dream man.

'*Twice* in Szeged,' the singer said.

'We would have made it to Budapest if it hadn't been for the Russians,' said the man who walked on his hands.

'Yes, it was the Russians who removed his shinbones!' said the dream man.

'Tell the truth,' the singer said. 'He was *born* without shinbones. But it's true that we couldn't get along with the Russians.'

'They tried to jail the bear,' said the dream man.

'Tell the truth,' Theobald said.

'We rescued his sister from them,' said the man who walked on his hands.

'So of course I must put them up,' said Herr Theobald, 'and they work as hard as they can. But who's interested in their act in this country? It's a Hungarian thing. There's no *tradition* of bears on unicycles here,' Theobald told us. 'And the damn dreams mean nothing to us Viennese.'

'Tell the truth,' said the dream man. 'It is because I have told the wrong dreams. We worked a nightclub on the Kärntnerstrasse, but then we got banned.'

'You should never have told *that* dream,' the singer said gravely.

'Well, it was your wife's responsibility, too!' the dream man said.

'She was *your* wife, then,' the singer said.

'Please stop it,' Theobald begged.

'We get to do the balls for children's diseases,' the dream man said. 'And some of the state hospitals – especially at Christmas.'

'If you would only do more with the bear,' Herr Theobald advised them.

'Speak to your sister about that,' said the singer. 'It's *her* bear – she's trained him, she's let him get lazy and sloppy and full of bad habits.'

'He is the only one of you who never makes fun of me,' said the man who could only walk on his hands.

'I would like to leave all this,' Grandmother said. 'This is, for me, an awful experience.'

'Please, dear lady,' Herr Theobald said, 'we only wanted to show you that we meant no offense. These are hard times. I need the B rating to attract more tourists, and I can't – in my heart – throw out the Circus Szolnok.'

'*In his heart,* my ass!' said the dream man. 'He's afraid of his sister. He wouldn't dream of throwing us out.'

'If he dreamed it, you would know it!' cried the man on his hands.

'I am afraid of the *bear*,' Herr Theobald said. 'It does everything she tells it to do.'

'Say "he," not "it,"' said the man on his hands. 'He is a fine bear, and he never hurt anybody. He has no claws, you know perfectly well – and very few teeth, either.'

'The poor thing has a terribly hard time eating,' Herr Theobald admitted. 'He is quite old, and he's messy.'

Over my father's shoulder, I saw him write in the giant pad: 'A depressed bear and an unemployed circus. This family is centered on the sister.'

At that moment out on the sidewalk, we could see her tending to the bear. It was early morning and the street was not especially busy. By law, of course, she had the bear on a leash, but it was a token control. In her startling red turban the woman walked up and down the sidewalk, following the lazy movements of the bear on his unicycle. The animal pedaled easily from parking meter to parking meter, sometimes leaning a paw on the meter as he turned. He was very talented on the unicycle, you could tell, but you could also tell that the unicycle was a dead end for him. You could see that the bear felt he could go no further with unicycling.

'She should bring him off the street now,' Herr Theobald fretted. 'The people in the pastry shop next door complain to me,' he told us. 'They say the bear drives their customers away.'

'That bear makes the customers *come*!' said the man on his hands.

'It makes some people come, it turns some away,' said the dream man. He was suddenly somber, as if his profundity had depressed him.

But we had been so taken up with the antics of the Circus Szolnok that we had neglected old Johanna. When my mother saw that Grandmother was quietly crying, she told me to bring the car around.

'It's been too much for her,' my father whispered to Theobald. The Circus Szolnok looked ashamed of themselves.

Outside on the sidewalk the bear pedaled up to me and handed me the keys; the car was parked at the curb. 'Not everyone likes to be given the keys in that fashion,' Herr Theobald told his sister.

'Oh, I thought he'd rather like it,' she said, rumpling my hair. She was as appealing as a barmaid, which

180

is to say that she was more appealing at night; in the daylight I could see that she was older than her brother, and older than her husbands too – and in time, I imagined, she would cease being lover and sister to them, respectively, and become a mother to them all. She was already a mother to the bear.

'Come over here,' she said to him. He pedaled listlessly in place on his unicycle, holding on to a parking meter for support. He licked the little glass face of the meter. She tugged his leash. He stared at her. She tugged again. Insolently, the bear began to pedal – first one way, then the next. It was as if he took interest, seeing that he had an audience. He began to show off.

'Don't try anything,' the sister said to him, but the bear pedaled faster and faster, going forward, going backward, angling sharply and veering among the parking meters; the sister had to let go of the leash. 'Duna, stop it!' she cried, but the bear was out of control. He let the wheel roll too close to the curb and the unicycle pitched him hard into the fender of a parked car. He sat on the sidewalk with the unicycle beside him; you could tell that he hadn't injured himself, but he looked very embarrassed and nobody laughed. 'Oh, Duna,' the sister said, scoldingly, but she went over and crouched beside him at the curb. 'Duna, Duna,' she reproved him, gently. He shook his big head; he would not look at her. There was some saliva strung on the fur near his mouth and she wiped this away with her hand. He pushed her hand away with his paw.

'Come back again!' cried Herr Theobald, miserably, as we got into our car.

Mother sat in the car with her eyes closed and her fingers massaging her temples; this way she seemed to hear nothing we said. She claimed it was her only defense against traveling with such a contentious family.

I did not want to report on the usual business concerning the care of the car, but I saw that Father was trying to maintain order and calm; he had the giant pad spread on his lap as if we'd just completed a routine investigation. 'What does the gauge tell us?' he asked.

'Someone put thirty-five kilometers on it,' I said.

'That terrible bear has been in here,' Grandmother said. 'There are hairs from the beast on the back seat, and I can *smell* him.'

'I don't smell anything,' Father said.

'And the perfume of that gypsy in the turban,' Grandmother said. 'It is hovering near the ceiling of the car.' Father and I sniffed. Mother continued to massage her temples.

On the floor by the brakes and clutch pedals I saw several of the mint-green toothpicks that the Hungarian singer was in the habit of wearing like a scar at the corner of his mouth. I didn't mention them. It was enough to imagine them all – out on the town, in our car. The singing driver, the man on his hands beside him – waving out the window with his feet. And in back, separating the dream man from his former wife – his great head brushing the upholstered roof, his mauling paws relaxed in his large lap – the old bear slouched like a benign drunk.

'Those poor people,' Mother said, her eyes still closed.

'Liars and criminals,' Grandmother said. 'Mystics and refugees and broken-down animals.'

'They were trying hard,' Father said, 'but they weren't coming up with the prizes.'

'Better off in a zoo,' said Grandmother.

'I had a good time,' Robo said.

'It's hard to break out of Class C,' I said.

'They have fallen past Z,' said old Johanna. 'They have disappeared from the human alphabet.'

'I think this calls for a letter,' Mother said.

But Father raised his hand — as if he were going to bless us — and we were quiet. He was writing in the giant pad and wished to be undisturbed. His face was stern. I knew that Grandmother felt confident of his verdict. Mother knew it was useless to argue. Robo was already bored. I steered us off through the tiny streets; I took Spiegelgasse to Lobkowitzplatz. Spiegelgasse is so narrow that you can see the reflection of your own car in the windows of the shops you pass, and I felt our movement through Vienna was superimposed (like that) — like a trick with a movie camera, as if we made a fairy-tale journey through a toy city.

When Grandmother was asleep in the car, Mother said, 'I don't suppose that in this case a change in the classification will matter very much, one way or another.'

'No,' Father said, 'not much at all.' He was right about that, though it would be years until I saw the Pension Grillparzer again.

When Grandmother died, rather suddenly and in her sleep, Mother announced that she was tired of traveling. The real reason, however, was that she began to find herself plagued by Grandmother's dream. 'The horses are so thin,' she told me once. 'I mean, I always knew they would be thin, but not *this* thin. And the soldiers — I knew they were miserable,' she said, 'but not *that* miserable.'

Father resigned from the Tourist Bureau and found a job with a local detective agency specializing in hotels and department stores. It was a satisfactory job for him, though he refused to work during the Christmas season – when, he said, some people ought to be allowed to steal a little.

My parents seemed to me to relax as they got older, and I really felt they were fairly happy near the end. I know that the strength of Grandmother's dream was dimmed by the *real* world, and specifically by what happened to Robo. He went to a private school and was well liked there, but he was killed by a homemade bomb in his first year at the university. He was not even 'political'. In his last letter to my parents he wrote: 'The self-seriousness of the radical factions among the students is much overrated. And the food is execrable.' Then Robo went to his history class, and his classroom was blown apart.

It was after my parents died that I gave up smoking and took up traveling again. I took my second wife back to the Pension Grillparzer. With my first wife, I never got as far as Vienna.

The Grillparzer had not kept Father's B rating very long, and it had fallen from the ratings altogether by the time I returned to it. Herr Theobald's sister was in charge of the place. Gone was her tart appeal and in its place was the sexless cynicism of some maiden aunts. She was shapeless and her hair was dyed a sort of bronze, so that her head resembled one of those copper scouring pads that you use on a pot. She did not remember me and was suspicious of my questions. Because I appeared to know so much about her past associates, she probably knew I was with the police.

The Hungarian singer had gone away – another woman thrilled by his voice. The dream man had been *taken* away – to an institution. His own dreams had turned to nightmares and he'd awakened the pension each night with his horrifying howls. His removal from the seedy premises, said Herr Theobald's sister, was almost simultaneous with the loss of the Grillparzer's B rating.

Herr Theobald was dead. He had dropped down clutching his heart in the hall, where he ventured one night to investigate what he thought was a prowler. It was only Duna, the malcontent bear, who was dressed in the dream man's pin-striped suit. Why Theobald's sister had dressed the bear in this fashion was not explained to me, but the shock of the sullen animal unicycling in the lunatic's left-behind clothes had been enough to scare Herr Theobald to death.

The man who could only walk on his hands had also fallen into the gravest trouble. His wristwatch snagged on a tine of an escalator and he was suddenly unable to hop off; his necktie, which he rarely wore because it dragged on the ground when he walked on his hands, was drawn under the step-off grate at the end of the escalator – where he was strangled. Behind him a line of people formed – marching in place by taking one step back and allowing the escalator to carry them forward, then taking another step back. It was quite a while before anyone got up the nerve to step over him. The world has many unintentionally cruel mechanisms that are not designed for people who walk on their hands.

After that, Theobald's sister told me, the Pension Grillparzer went from Class C to much worse. As the burden of management fell more heavily on her, she had less time for Duna and the bear grew senile and indecent in his habits. Once he bullied a mailman down a marble staircase at such a ferocious pace that the man fell and broke his hip: the attack was reported and an old city ordinance forbidding unrestrained animals in places open to the public was enforced. Duna was outlawed at the Pension Grillparzer.

For a while, Theobald's sister kept the bear in a cage in the courtyard of the building, but he was taunted by dogs and children, and food (and worse) was dropped into his cage from the apartments that faced the courtyard. He grew unbearlike and devious – only pretending to sleep – and he ate most of someone's cat. Then he was poisoned twice and became afraid to eat anything in this perilous environment. There was no alternative but to donate him to the Schönbrunn Zoo, but there was even some doubt as to his acceptability. He was toothless and ill, perhaps contagious, and his long history of having been treated as a human being did not prepare him for the gentler routine of zoo life.

His outdoor sleeping quarters in the courtyard of the Grillparzer had inflamed his rheumatism, and even his one talent, unicycling, was irretrievable. When he first tried it in the zoo, he fell. Someone laughed. Once anyone laughed at something Duna did, Theobald's sister explained, Duna would never do that thing again. He became, at last, a kind of charity case at Schönbrunn, where he died a short two months after he'd taken up his new lodgings. In the opinion of Theobald's sister, Duna died of mortification – the result of a rash that spread over his great chest, which then had to be shaved. A shaved bear, one zoo official said, is embarrassed to death.

In the cold courtyard of the building I looked in the bear's empty cage. The birds hadn't left a fruit seed, but in a corner of his cage was a looming mound of the bear's ossified droppings – as void of life, and even odor, as the corpses captured by the holocaust at Pompeii. I couldn't help thinking of Robo; of the bear, there were more remains.

In the car I was further depressed to notice that not one kilometer had been added to the gauge, not one kilometer had been driven in secret. There was no-one around to take liberties anymore.

'When we're a safe distance away from your precious Pension Grillparzer,' my second wife said to me, 'I'd like you to tell me why you brought me to such a shabby place.'

'It's a long story,' I admitted.

I was thinking I had noticed a curious lack of either enthusiasm or bitterness in the account of the world by Theobald's sister. There was in her story the flatness one associates with a storyteller who is accepting of unhappy endings, as if her life and her companions had never been exotic to *her* – as if they had always been staging a ludicrous and doomed effort at reclassification.

# THE KING OF
# THE NOVEL

## 1. Why I Like Charles Dickens; Why Some People Don't

*Great Expectations* is the first novel I read that made me wish I had written it; it is the novel that made me want to be a novelist – specifically, to move a reader as I was moved then. I believe that *Great Expectations* has the most wonderful and most perfectly worked-out plot for a novel in the English language; at the same time, it never deviates from its intention to move you to laughter and to tears. But there is more than one thing about this novel that some people don't like – and there is one thing in particular that they don't like about Dickens in general. Here is the thing highest on the list that they don't like: the intention of a novel by Charles Dickens is to move you emotionally, not intellectually; and it is by emotional means that Dickens intends to influence you socially. Dickens is not an analyst; his writing is not analytical – although it can be didactic. His genius is descriptive; he can describe a thing so vividly – and so influentially – that no-one can look at that thing in the same way again.

You cannot encounter the prisons in Dickens's novels and ever again feel completely self-righteous about prisoners being where they belong; you cannot encounter a lawyer of Mr Jaggers's terrifying ambiguity and ever again put yourself willingly in a lawyer's hands – Jaggers, although only a minor character in *Great Expectations,* may be our literature's greatest indictment of living by abstract rules. Dickens has even provided me with a lasting vision of a critic; he is Bentley Drummle, 'the next heir but one to a baronetcy', and 'so sulky a fellow that he even took up a book as if its writer had done him an injury'.

Although his personal experiences with social evil had been brief and youthful, they never ceased to haunt Dickens – the humiliation of his father in the debtors' prison at Marshalsea; his own three months' labor (at age eleven) in a blacking warehouse at Hungerford Stairs, pasting labels on bottles; and because of his father's money problems, the family's several moves – especially, when Charles was nine, to meaner accommodations in Chatham; and shortly thereafter, away from the Chatham of his childhood. 'I thought that life was sloppier than I expected to find it,' he wrote. Yet his imagination was never impoverished; in *David Copperfield,* he wrote (remembering his life as a reader in his attic room at St Mary's Place, Chatham), 'I have been Tom Jones (a child's Tom Jones, a harmless creature).' He had *been* Don Quixote, too – and all the even less likely heroes of the Victorian fairy tales of his time. As Harry Stone has written: 'It is hard to know which came first, Dickens's interest in fairy tales or his conditioning by them.' Dickens's fine biographer,

Edgar Johnson, describes the sources of the author's imagination similarly, claiming further that Dickens had devised 'a new literary form, a kind of fairy tale that is at once humorous, heroic, and realistic'.

The Chatham of Dickens's childhood is sharply recalled in *Great Expectations* – in the churchyard graves he could see from his attic room, and in the black convict hulk, 'like a wicked Noah's ark,' which he saw looming offshore on the boating trips he took up the Medway to the Thames; that is where he saw his first convicts, too. So much of the landscape of *Great Expectations* is Chatham's landscape, the foggy marshes, the river mist; and his real-life model for the Blue Boar was there in nearby Rochester, and Uncle Pumblechook's house was there – and Satis House, where Miss Havisham lives. On walks with his father, from Gravesend to Rochester, they would pause in Kent and view the mansion atop a two-mile slope called Gad's Hill; his father told him that if he was very hardworking, he might get to live there one day. Given his family's Chatham circumstances, this must have been hard for young Charles to believe, but he did get to live there one day – for the last twelve years of his life; he wrote *Great Expectations* there, and he died there. For readers who find Dickens's imagination farfetched, they should look at his life.

His was an imagination fueled by personal unhappiness and the zeal of a social reformer. Like many successful people, he made good use of disappointments – responding to them with energy, with near-frenzied activity, rather than needing to recover from them. At fifteen, he left school; at seventeen, he was a law reporter; at nineteen, a parliamentary reporter. At twenty, he was a witness to the unemployment, starvation, and cholera of the winter of 1831–2 – and his first literary success, at twenty-one, was made gloomy by the heartbreak of his first love. She was a banker's daughter whose family shunned Dickens; years later, she returned to him in her embarrassing maturity – she was plump and tiresome, then, and he shunned her. But when he first met her, her rejection made him work all the harder; Dickens never moped.

He had what Edgar Johnson calls a 'boundless confidence in the power of the will'. One of his earliest reviews (by his future father-in-law; imagine that!) was absolutely right about the talents of the young author. 'A close observer of character and manners,' George Hogarth wrote about the twenty-four-year-old Dickens, 'with a strong sense of the ridiculous and a graphic faculty of placing in the most whimsical and amusing lights the follies and absurdities of human nature. He has the power, too, of producing tears as well as laughter. His pictures of the vices and wretchedness which abound in this vast city are sufficient to strike the heart of the most careless and insensitive reader.'

Indeed, Dickens's young star so outshone that of Robert Seymour, the *Pickwick Papers'* first illustrator, that Seymour blew his brains out with a muzzle-loader. By 1837 Dickens was already famous for Mr Pickwick. He was only twenty-five; he even took command of his hapless parents; having twice bailed his father out of debtors' prison, Dickens moved his parents forcibly from London to Exeter – an attempt to prevent his feckless father from running up an unpayable tab in his famous son's name.

Dickens's watchdog behavior regarding the social ills of his time could best be described, politically, as reform liberalism; yet he was not to be pinned down.

His stance for the abolition of the death penalty, for example, was based on his belief that the punishment of death did nothing to deter crime – not out of sentiment for any malefactor. For Dickens, 'the major evil' – as Johnson describes it – 'was the psychological effect of the horrible drama of hanging before a brutalized and gloating mob'. He was tireless in his support of reform homes for women, and of countless services and charities for the poor; by the time of *Dombey and Son* (1846–8), he had a firmly developed ethic regarding the human greed evident in the world of competitive business – and a strongly expressed moral outrage at the indifference shown to the welfare of the downtrodden; he had begun to see, past *Oliver Twist* (1837–9), that vice and cruelty were not randomly bestowed on individuals at birth but were the creations of society. And well before the time of *Bleak House* (1852–3), he had tenacious hold of the knowledge that 'it is better to suffer a great wrong than to have recourse to the much greater wrong of the law'.

He was thirty when he had his first fling at editing 'a great liberal newspaper', dedicated to the 'Principles of Progress and Improvement, of Education, Civil and Religious Liberty, and Equal Legislation'; he lasted only seventeen days. With *Household Words,* he did much better; the magazine was as successful as many of his novels, full of what he called 'social wonders, good and evil'. Among the first to admire the writing of George Eliot, he was also among the first to guess her sex. 'I have observed what seem to me to be such womanly touches,' he wrote to her, 'that the assurance on the title-page is insufficient to satisfy me, even now. If they originated with no woman, I believe that no man ever before had the art of making himself, mentally, so like a woman, since the world began.' Of course, she was charmed – and she confessed to him.

He was so industrious that (despite his generosity) even the work of his own friends failed to impress him. 'There is a horrid respectability about the most of the best of them,' he wrote, '—a little, finite, systematic routine in them, strangely expressive to me of the state of England herself.' Yet he was ever the champion of the un-championed – as in Mr Sleary's heartfelt and lisped plea for the circus artists in *Hard Times*. 'Don't be croth with uth poor vagabondth. People must be amuthed. They can't be alwayth a learning, nor yet can they be alwayth a working, they ain't made for it. You *mutht* have uth, Thquire. Do the withe thing and the kind thing, too, and make the betht of uth; not the wortht!' It is this quality in Dickens that has been blessed by Irving Howe, who writes that 'in [his] strongest novels, entertainer and moralist come to seem shadows of one another – finally two voices out of the same mouth.'

Dickens's gift is how spontaneously he can render a situation both sympathetic and hilarious – and charged with his fierce indignation, with what Johnson calls his 'furious exposure of social evils'. Yet Dickens's greatest risk-taking, as a writer, has little to do with his social morality. What he is most unafraid of is sentimentality – of anger, of passion, of emotionally and psychologically revealing himself; he is not self-protective; he is never careful. In the present, post-modernist praise of the *craft* of writing – of the subtle, of the exquisite – we may have refined the very heart out of the novel. Dickens would have had more fun with today's literary elitists and minimalists than he had with Mr Pumblechook and Mrs Jellyby. He was the king of the novel in that century which produced the models of the form.

Dickens wrote great comedy – high and low – and he wrote great melodrama. At the conclusion of the first stage of Pip's expectations, Dickens writes: 'Heaven knows we need never be ashamed of our tears, for they are rain upon the blinding dust of earth, overlying our hard hearts.' But we *are* ashamed of our tears. We live at a time when critical taste tells us that to be softhearted is akin to doltishness; we're so influenced by the junk on television that even in reacting against it, we overreact – we conclude that *any* attempt to move an audience to laughter or to tears is shameless, is either sitcom or soap opera or both.

Edgar Johnson is correct in observing that 'though much has been said about Victorian restraint, emotionally it is we who are restrained, not they. Large bodies of modern readers, especially those called "sophisticated", distrust any uncurbed yielding to emotion. Above all when the emotion is noble, heroic, or tender, they wince in skeptical suspicion or distaste. A heartfelt expression of sentiment seems to them exaggerated, hypocritical, or embarrassing.' And Johnson offers a reason for this. 'There are explanations, of course, for our peculiar fear of sentiment as sentimental. With the enormous growth of popular fiction, vulgar imitators have cheapened the methods they learned from great writers and coarsened their delineation of emotion. Dickens's very powers marked him out as a model for such emulation.'

To the modern reader, too often when a writer risks being sentimental, the writer is already guilty. But as a writer it is cowardly to so fear sentimentality that one avoids it altogether. It is typical – and forgivable

– among student writers to avoid being mush-minded by simply refusing to write about people, or by refusing to subject characters to emotional extremes. A short story about a four-course meal from the point of view of a fork will never be sentimental; it may never matter very much to us, either. Dickens took sentimental risks with abandon. 'His weapons were those of caricature and burlesque,' Johnson writes, 'of melodrama and unrestrained sentiment.'

And here's another wonderful thing about him: his writing is never vain – I mean that he never sought to be original. He never pretended to be an explorer, discovering neglected evils. Nor was he so vain as to imagine that his love or his use of the language was particularly special; he could write very prettily when he wanted to, but he never had so little to say that he thought the object of writing was pretty language; he did not care about being original in that way, either. The broadest novelists never cared for that kind of original language – Dickens, Hardy, Tolstoy, Hawthorne, Melville . . . their so-called style is every style; they use all styles. To such novelists, originality with language is mere fashion; it will pass. The larger, plainer things – the things they are preoccupied with, their obsessions – these will last: the story, the characters, the laughter and the tears.

Yet writers who are considered masters of style have also marveled at Dickens's technical brilliance, while recognizing it as instinctual – as nothing anyone ever learned, or could be taught. G. K. Chesterton's *Charles Dickens: A Critical Study* is both an appreciative and precise view of Dickens's techniques; Chesterton also offers a marvelous defense of Dickens's characters. 'Though his characters often were caricatures, they were not such caricatures as was supposed by those who had never met such characters,' Chesterton writes. 'And the critics had never met the characters; because the critics did not live the common life of the English people; and Dickens did. England was a much more amusing and horrible place than it appeared to the sort of man who wrote reviews.'

It is worth noting that both Johnson and Chesterton stress Dickens's fondness for the *common;* Dickens's critics stress his eccentricity. 'There can be no question of the importance of Dickens as a human event in history,' Chesterton writes, '. . . a naked flame of mere genius, breaking out in a man without culture, without tradition, without help from historic religions and philosophies or from the great foreign schools; and revealing a light that never was on sea or land, if only the long fantastic shadows that it threw from common things.'

Vladimir Nabokov has pointed out that Dickens didn't write every sentence as if his reputation depended on it. 'When Dickens has some information to impart to his reader through conversation or meditation, the imagery is generally not conspicuous,' Nabokov writes. Dickens knew how to keep a reader reading; he trusted his descriptive powers – as much as he trusted his ability to make his readers feel emotionally connected to his characters. Very simply, narrative momentum and emotional interest in the characters are what make a novel more compellingly readable on page 300 than it is on page 30. 'The bursts of vivid imagery are spaced' is how Nabokov puts it.

But didn't he exaggerate everything? his critics ask.

'When people say that Dickens exaggerates,' George Santayana writes, 'it seems to me that they have no eyes and no ears. They probably have only *notions* of what things and people are; they accept them conventionally, at their diplomatic value.' And to those who contend that no-one was ever so sentimental, or that there was no-one ever *like* Wemmick or Jaggers or Bentley Drummle, Santayana says: 'The polite world is lying; there *are* such people; we are such people ourselves in our true moments.' Santayana also defends Dickens's stylistic excesses: 'This faculty, which renders him a consummate comedian, is just what alienated him from a later generation in which people of taste were aesthetes and virtuous people were higher snobs; they wanted a mincing art, and he gave them copious improvisation, they wanted analysis and development, and he gave them absolute comedy.'

No wonder that – both because of and in spite of his popularity – Dickens was frequently misunderstood, and often mocked. In his first visit to America he was relentless in his attack on America's practice of ignoring international copyright; he also detested slavery, and said so, and he found loathsome and crude the American habit of *spitting* – according to Dickens, practically everywhere! For his criticism he was rewarded by our critics, who called him a 'flash reporter' and 'that famous penny-a-liner'; his mind was described as 'coarse, vulgar, impudent, and superficial'; he was called 'narrow-minded' and 'conceited,' and among all visitors, ever, to 'this original and remarkable country,' he was regarded as 'the most flimsy – the most childish – the most trashy – the most contemptible . . .'

So, of course, Dickens had enemies; they could not touch his splendid instincts, or match his robust life. Before beginning *Great Expectations,* he said, 'I must make the most I can out of the book – I think a good name?' Good, indeed, and a title many writers wish were free for them to use, a title many wonderful novels could have had: *The Great Gatsby, To the Lighthouse, The Mayor of Casterbridge, The Sun Also Rises, Anna Karenina, Moby Dick* – all great expectations, of course.

## 2. A Prisoner of Marriage; The 'One Happiness I Have Missed in Life . . .'

But what about the plot? his critics ask. Aren't his plots unlikely?

Oh, boy; are they ever 'unlikely'! I wonder how many people who call a plot 'unlikely' ever realize that they do not like any plot at all. The nature of plot *is* unlikely. And if you've been reading a great many contemporary novels, you're probably unused to encountering much in the way of plot there; should you encounter one now, you'd be sure to find it unlikely. Yet when the British sailed off to their little war with Argentina in 1982, they used the luxury liner, the *Queen Elizabeth II,* as a troop transport. And what became the highest military priority of the Argentinian forces, who were quite overpowered in this war? To sink that luxury liner, the *Queen Elizabeth II*, of course – to salvage, at the very least, what people call a 'moral victory'. Imagine that! But we accept far more unlikely events in the news than we accept in fiction. Fiction is, and has to be, better made than the news; plots, even the most unlikely ones, are better made than real life, too.

Let us look at Charles Dickens's marriage for a moment; the story of his marriage, were we to encounter it in any novel, would seem highly unlikely to us. When Dickens married Catherine Hogarth, Catherine's younger sister Mary, who was only sixteen, moved in with them; Mary adored her sister's husband, and she was an ever-cheerful presence in their house – perhaps seeming all the more good-natured and even-tempered alongside Catherine's periods of sullen withdrawal. How much easier it is to be a visitor than to be a spouse; and to make matters worse, Mary died at seventeen, thus perfectly enshrining herself in Dickens's memory – and becoming, in the later years of his marriage to Kate (Catherine was called Kate), an even more impossible idol, against whom poor Kate could never compete. Mary was a vision of perfection as girlish innocence, of course, and she would appear and re-appear in Dickens's novels – she is Little Nell in *The Old Curiosity Shop*, she is Agnes in *David Copperfield*, she is Little Dorrit. Surely her goodness finds its way into Biddy in *Great Expectations*, too, although Biddy's capabilities for criticizing Pip come from stronger stuff than anything Dickens would have had the occasion to encounter in Mary Hogarth.

In his first visit to America, while Dickens made few references to the strains that Kate felt while traveling (her anxieties for the children back in England, especially), he did observe the profound lack of interest in America that was expressed by Kate's maid. Kate herself, he documented – in the course of getting on and off boats and coaches and trains – had fallen 743 times. Although this was surely an exaggeration, Mrs Dickens did compile an impressive record of clumsiness; Johnson suggests that she suffered from a nervous disorder, for her lack of physical control was remarkable. Dickens once cast her in one of his amateur theatrical company's performances – it was a small part in which Kate spoke a total of only thirty lines; yet she managed to fall through a trapdoor on stage and so severely sprained her ankle that she had to be replaced. It seems an extreme step to take to gain Dickens's attention; but Kate surely suffered their marriage in her own way as acutely as her husband did in his.

When Dickens's twenty-three-year-old marriage to Kate was floundering, who would be living with them but another of Kate's younger sisters? Dickens found Georgina 'the most admirable and affectionate of girls'; and such was her loyalty to him that after Dickens and Kate separated, Georgina remained with Dickens. She might have been in love with him, and quite more to him than a help with the children (Kate bore Dickens ten children), but there is nothing to suggest that their relationship was sexual – although, at the time, they were subject to gossip about that.

At the time of his separation from Kate, Dickens was probably in love with an eighteen-year-old actress in his amateur theatrical company – her name was Ellen Ternan. When Kate discovered a bracelet that Dickens had intended as a present for Ellen (he was in the habit of giving little gifts to his favorite performers), Kate accused him of having already consummated a relationship with Ellen – a relationship that, in all likelihood, was not consummated until some years after Dickens and Kate had separated. (Dickens's relationship with Ellen Ternan must have been nearly as guilt ridden and unhappy as his marriage.) At the time of the separation, Kate's mother spread the rumor that Dickens had already taken Ellen Ternan as his mistress. Dickens published a statement under the headline 'PERSONAL' on the front page of his own, very popular magazine *(Household Words)* that such 'misrepresentations' of his character were 'most grossly false'. Dickens's self-righteousness in his own defense invited controversy; every detail of his marriage and separation was published in the New York *Tribune* and in all the English newspapers. Imagine that!

It was 1858. Within three years, Dickens would change the name of *Household Words* to *All the Year Round* and continue his exhausting habit of serializing his novels for his magazine; he would begin the great numbers of fervent public readings that would undermine his health (he would give more than four hundred readings before his death in 1870); and he would complete both *A Tale of Two Cities* and *Great Expectations.* 'I am incapable of rest,' he told his best and oldest friend, John Forster. 'I am quite confident I should rust, break, and die, if I spared myself. Much better to die, doing.'

As for love: he would lament that a true love was the 'one happiness I have missed in life, and the one friend and companion I never made'. More than a little of that melancholic conviction would haunt Pip's quest of Estella's love (and profoundly influence Dickens's first version of the ending of *Great Expectations).* And the slowness and the coldness with which the teenaged Ellen Ternan responded to the famous author in his late forties would cause Dickens to know more than a little of what Pip's longing for Estella was.

His marriage to Kate had, in his view, been a prison; but in taking leave of it, he had encountered a most public scandal and humiliation, and a reluctant mistress – the relationship with Ellen Ternan would never be joyously celebrated. The lovelessness of his marriage would linger with him – just as the dust of the debtors' prison would pursue Mr Dorrit, just as the cold mists of the marshes would follow young Pip to London, just as the 'taunt' of Newgate wold hang over Pip when he so hopefully meets Estella's coach.

Pip is another of Dickens's orphans, but he is never so pure as Oliver Twist and never as nice as David Copperfield. He is not only a young man with unrealistic expectations; he is a young brat who adopts the superior manners of a gentleman (an unearned position) while detesting his lowly origins and feeling ashamed in the company of men of a higher social class than his. Pip is a snob. 'It is a most miserable thing to feel ashamed of home,' he admits; yet as he sets out to London to enjoy his unknown benefactor's provisions, Pip heaps 'a gallon of condescension upon everybody in the village'.

It must have been a time of self-doubt for Dickens – at least, he suffered some reevaluation of his self-esteem. He had kept his work days in the blacking warehouse a secret from his own children. Although his origins were not so lowly as young Pip's, Dickens must have thought them low enough. He would never forget how deeply his spirits sank when he was pasting labels on the bottles at Hungerford Stairs.

And was he feeling guilty, too, and considering some of his own ventures to have only the airs of a gentleman (without real substance) about them? Surely the patrician goals to which young Pip aspires are held in some contempt in *Great Expectations*; the mysterious and elaborate provisions that enable Pip to 'live smooth', to 'be above work'. At the end – as there is often at the end, with Dickens – there is a softening of the heart; the work ethic, that bastion of the middle class, is graciously given some respect. 'We were not in a grand way of business,' Pip says of his job, 'but we had a good name, and worked for our profits, and did very well.' This is an example of what Chesterton means: that 'Dickens did not write what the people wanted. Dickens wanted what the people wanted.' This is an important distinction, especially when regarding Dickens's popularity; the man did not write *for* an audience so much as he expressed an audience's hunger – he made astonishingly vivid what an audience feared, what it dreamed of, what it wanted.

In our time, it is often necessary to defend a writer's popularity; from time to time, in literary fashion, it is considered bad taste to be popular – if a writer is popular, how can he be any good? And it is frequently the role of lesser wits to demean the accomplishments of writers with more sizable audiences, and reputations, than their own. Oscar Wilde, for example, was a teenager when Dickens died; regarding Dickens's sentiment, Wilde remarked that 'it would take a heart of steel not to laugh at the death of Little Nell.' It was also Wilde who said that Flaubert's conversation was on a level with the conversation of a pork butcher; but Flaubert was not in the conversation business – which, in time, may prove to be Wilde's most lasting contribution to our literature. Compared to Dickens or Flaubert, Wilde's *writing* is on a level with pork butchery. Chesterton, who was born four years after Dickens's death and who occupied a literary period wherein popularity (for a writer) was suspect, dismissed the *charges* against Dickens's popularity very bluntly. History would have to pay attention to Dickens, Chesterton said – because, quite simply, 'the man led a mob.'

Dickens was abundant and magnificent with description, with the atmosphere surrounding everything – and with the tactile, with every detail that was terrifying or viscerally *felt.* Those were among his strengths as a writer; and if there were weaknesses, too, they are more easily spotted in his endings than in his beginnings or middles. In the end, like a good Christian, he wants to forgive. Enemies shake hands (or even marry!); every orphan finds a family. Miss Havisham, who is a truly terrible woman, cries out to Pip, whom she has manipulated and deceived, 'Who am I, for God's sake, that I should be kind?' Yet when she begs his forgiveness, he forgives her. Magwitch, regardless of how he 'lived rough', is permitted to die with a smile on his lips, secure in the knowledge that his lost daughter is alive. Talk about *unlikely*! Pip's horrible sister finally dies, thus allowing the dear Joe to marry a truly good woman. And, in the revised ending, Pip's unrequited love is rectified; he sees 'no shadow of another parting' from Estella. This is mechanical matchmaking; it is not realistic; it is overly tidy as if the neatness of the *form* of the novel requires that all the characters be brought together. This may seem, to our cynical expectations, unduly hopeful.

The hopefulness that makes everyone love *A Christmas Carol* draws fire when Dickens employs it in *Great Expectations;* when Christmas is over, Dickens's hopefulness strikes many as mere wishful thinking. Dickens's original ending to *Great Expectations,* that Pip and his impossible love, Estella, should stay apart, is thought by most modern critics to be the proper (and certainly the modern) conclusion – from which Dickens eventually shied away; for such a change of heart and mind, he is accused of selling out. After an early manhood of shallow goals, Pip is meant finally to see the falseness of his values – and of Estella – and he emerges a sadder though a wiser fellow. Many readers have expressed the belief that Dickens stretches credulity too far when he leads us to suppose – in his revised ending – that Estella and Pip could be happy ever after; or that anyone can. Of his new ending – where Pip and Estella are reconciled – Dickens himself remarked to a friend: 'I have put in a very pretty piece of writing, and I have no doubt that the story will be more acceptable through the alteration.' That Estella would make Pip – or anyone – a rotten wife is not the point. 'Don't be afraid of my being a blessing to him,' she slyly tells Pip, who is bemoaning her choice of a first husband. The point is, Estella and Pip are linked; fatalistically, they belong to each other – happily or unhappily.

Although the suggestion that Dickens revise the original ending came from his friend Bulwer-Lytton, who wished the book to close on a happier note, Edgar Johnson wisely points out that 'the changed ending reflected a desperate hope that Dickens could not banish from within his own heart.' That hope is not a last-minute alteration, tacked on, but simply the culmination of a hope that abides throughout the novel: that Estella might change. After all, Pip changes (he is the first major character in a Dickens novel who changes realistically, albeit slowly). The book isn't called *Great Expectations* for nothing. It is not, I think, meant to be an entirely bitter title – although I can undermine my own argument by reminding myself that we first hear that Pip is 'a young fellow of great expectations' from the ominous and cynical Mr Jaggers, that veteran hard-liner who will, quite rightfully, warn Pip to 'take nothing on its looks; take everything on evidence. There's no better rule.' But that was never Dickens's rule. Mr Gradgrind, from *Hard Times,* believed in nothing and possessed nothing but the facts; yet it is Mr Sleary's advice that Dickens heeds, to 'do the withe thing and the kind thing too.' It is both the kind and the 'withe' thing that Pip and Estella end up together.

In fact, it is the first ending that is out of character – for Dickens and for the novel. Pip, upon meeting Estella (after two years of hearing only rumors of her), remarks with a pinched heart: 'I was very glad afterwards to have had the interview, for in her face and in her voice, and in her touch, she gave me the assurance that suffering had been stronger than Miss Havisham's teaching, and had given her a heart to understand what my heart used to be.' Although that tone – superior and self-pitying – is more modern than Dickens's romantic revision, I fail to see how we or our literature would be better off for it. There is a contemporary detachment in it, even a smugness. Remember this about Charles Dickens: he was active and exuberant when he was happy; he was twice as busy when he was unhappy. In the first ending, Pip is moping; Dickens never moped.

The revised ending reads: 'I took her hand in mine, and we went out of the ruined place; and as the morning mists had risen long ago when I first left the forge, so the evening mists were rising now, and in all the broad expanse of tranquil light they showed to me, I saw no shadow of another parting from her.' A very pretty piece of writing, as Dickens noted, and eternally open – still ambiguous (Pip's hopes have been dashed before) – and far more the mirror of the quality of trust in the novel as a whole. It is that hopeful ending that sings with all the rich contradiction we should love Dickens for; it both underlines and undermines everything before it. Pip is basically good, basically gullible; he starts out being human, he learns by error

– and by becoming ashamed of himself – and he keeps on being human. That touching illogic seems not only generous but true.

'I loved her simply because I found her irresistible,' Pip says miserably; and of falling in love, in general, he observes, 'How could I, a poor dazed village lad, avoid that wonderful inconsistency into which the best and wisest of men fall every day?' And what does Miss Havisham have to tell us about love? 'I'll tell you what real love is,' she says. 'It is blind devotion, unquestioning self-humiliation, utter submission, trust and belief against yourself and against the whole world, giving up your whole heart and soul to the smiter – as I did!'

In her jilted fury, Miss Havisham wears her wedding dress the rest of her life and, by her own admission, replaces Estella's heart with ice – to make Estella all the more capable of destroying the men in her life as savagely as Miss Havisham was destroyed. Miss Havisham is one of the greatest witches in the history of fairy tales, because she actually is what she first seems. She appears more wicked and cruel to Pip when he meets her than that runaway convict who has accosted Pip as a child on the marshes; later, she greedily enjoys Pip's misunderstanding (that she is not the witch he first thought her to be, but an eccentric fairy godmother). She knows he is mistaken, yet she encourages him; her evil is complicitous. In the end, of course, she turns out to be the witch she always was. This is real magic, real fairy-tale stuff – but the eccentricity of Miss Havisham, to many of Dickens's critics, makes her one of his least believable characters.

It might surprise his critics to know that Miss Havisham did not spring wholly from his imagination.

In his youth, he would often see a madwoman on Oxford Street, about whom he wrote an essay for his magazine, *Household Words.* He called the essay 'Where We Stopped Growing,' in which he described 'the White Woman . . . dressed entirely in white . . . With white boots, we know she picks her way through the winter dirt. She is a conceited old creature, cold and formal in manner, and evidently went simpering mad on personal grounds alone – no doubt because a wealthy Quaker wouldn't marry her. This is her bridal dress. She is always . . . on her way to church to marry the false Quaker. We observe in her mincing step and fishy eye that she intends to lead him a sharp life. We stopped growing when we got at the conclusion that the Quaker had had a happy escape of the White Woman.' This was written several years before *Great Expectations.* Three years before that he had published in a monthly supplement to *Household Words* (called *Household Narrative)* a true-life account of a woman who sets herself on fire with a lit Christmas tree; she is saved from death, but severely burned, when a young man throws her to the floor and wraps her up in a rug – Miss Havisham's burning, and Pip's rescue of her, almost exactly.

Dickens was not so much a fanciful and whimsical inventor of unlikely characters and situations as he was a relentlessly keen witness of the real-life victims of his time; he sought out the sufferers, the people seemingly singled out by Fate or rendered helpless by their society – not those people complacently escaping the disasters of their time but the people who stood in the face of or on the edge of those disasters. The accusations against him that he was a sensationalist are the accusations of conventionally secure and smug people – certain that the mainstream of life is both safe and right, and therefore the only life that's true.

'The key of the great characters of Dickens,' Chesterton writes, 'is that they are all great fools. There is the same difference between a great fool and a small fool as there is between a great poet and a small poet. The great fool is a being who is above wisdom and not below it.' A chief and riveting characteristic of 'the great fool' is, of course, his capacity for destruction – for self-destruction, too, but for all kinds of havoc making. Look at Shakespeare: think of Lear, Hamlet, Othello – they were *all* 'great fools,' of course.

And there is one course that the great fools of literature often seem to follow without hesitation; they are trapped by their own lies, and/or by their vulnerability to the lies of others. In a story with a great fool in it, there's almost inevitably a great lie. Of course, the most important dishonesty in *Great Expectations* is Miss Havisham's; hers is a lie of omission. And Pip lies to his sister and Joe about his first visit to Miss Havisham's; he tells them that Miss Havisham keeps 'a black velvet coach' in her house, and that they all pretended to ride on this stationary coach while four 'immense' dogs 'fought for veal-cutlets out of a silver basket'. Little can Pip know that his lie is less extraordinary than what will prove to be the truth of Miss Havisham's life in Satis House, and the connections with her life that Pip will encounter in the so-called outside world.

The convict Magwitch, who threatens young Pip's life, and his liver, in the book's opening pages, will turn out to have a more noble heart than our young hero has. 'A man who had been soaked in water, and smothered in mud and lamed by stones, and cut by flints, and stung by nettles, and torn by briars; who limped, and shivered, and glared, and growled' – a man whom Pip sees disappearing on the marshes in the vicinity of 'a gibbet, with some chains hanging to it which had once held a pirate . . . as if he were the pirate come to life, and come down, and [was] going back to hook himself up again' – that this same man will later be a model of honor is part of the great mischief, the pure fun, of the plot of *Great Expectations*. Plot is entertainment to Dickens, it is pure pleasure-giving to an audience – enhanced by the fact that most of his novels were serialized; great and surprising coincidences were among the gifts he gave to his serial readers. A critic who scoffs at the chance meetings and other highly circumstantial developments in a Dickens narrative must have a most underdeveloped sense of enjoyment.

Unashamedly, Dickens wrote *to* his readers. He chides them, he seduces them, he shocks them; he gives them slapstick and sermons. It was his aim, Johnson says 'not to turn the stomach but to move the heart'. But it is my strong suspicion that in a contemporary world, where hearts are far more hardened, Dickens would have been motivated to turn the stomach, too – as the one means remaining for reaching those hardened hearts. He was shameless in that aim; he cajoled his audiences; he gave them great pleasure so that they would also keep their eyes open and not look away from his visions of the grotesque, from his nearly constant moral outrage.

In *Great Expectations,* maybe he felt he had given Pip and Estella – and his readers – enough pain. Why not give Pip and Estella to each other at the end? Charles Dickens would never find that 'one happiness I have missed in life, and the one friend and companion I never made'. But to Pip he would give that pleasure; he would give Pip his Estella.

### 3. 'No Help or Pity in All the Glittering Multitude'; in 'the Ruined Garden'

But what about the *plot*? his critics keep asking. How can you believe it?

Very simply: just accept as a fact that everyone of any emotional importance to you is related to everyone else of any emotional importance to you; these relationships need not extend to blood, of course, but the people who change your life emotionally – all those people, from different places, from different times, spanning many wholly unrelated coincidences – are nonetheless 'related'. We associate people with each other for emotional not for factual reasons – people who've never met each other, who don't know each other exist; people, even, who have forgotten us. In a novel by Charles Dickens, such people really *are* related – sometimes, even, by blood; almost always by circumstances, by coincidences; and most of all by plot. Look at what a force Miss Havisham is: anyone of any importance to Pip turns out to have (or have had) some kind of relationship with her!

Miss Havisham is so willfully deceptive, so deliberately evil. She is far worse than a vicious old woman made nasty and peculiar by her own hysterical egotism (although she is that, too); she is actively engaged in *seducing* Pip – she consciously intends for Estella to torment him. If you are so unimaginative that you believe such people don't exist, you must at least acknowledge that we (most of us) are as capable as Pip of allowing ourselves to be seduced. Pip is warned;

Estella herself warns him. The story is not so much about Miss Havisham's absolute evil as it is about Pip's expectations overriding his common sense. Pip wants to be a gentleman; he wants Estella – and his ambitions guide him more forcefully than his perceptions. Isn't this a failing we can recognize within ourselves?

Do not quarrel with Dickens for his excesses. The weaknesses in *Great Expectations* are few, and they are weaknesses of underdoing – not overdoing. The rather quickly assumed friendship, almost instant, between Pip and Herbert is never really developed or very strongly felt; we are supposed to take Herbert's absolute goodness for granted (it is never very engagingly demonstrated) – and that Herbert's nickname for Pip is 'Handel' drives me crazy! I find Herbert's goodness much harder to take than Miss Havisham's evil. And Dickens's love for amateur theatrical performers overreaches his ability to make Mr Wopsle and that poor fool's ambitions interesting. Chapters 30 and 31 are boring; perhaps they were hastily written, or else they represent a lapse in Dickens's own interest. For whatever reason, they are surely not examples of his notorious overwriting; everything that he overdid, he at least did with boundless energy.

Johnson writes that 'Dickens liked and disliked people; he was never merely indifferent. He loved and laughed and derided and despised and hated; he never patronized or sniffed.' Witness Orlick: he is as dangerous as a mistreated dog; there is little sympathy for the social circumstances underlying Orlick's villainy; he's a bad one, plain and simple – he means to kill. Witness Joe: proud, honest, hardworking, uncomplaining, and manifesting endless good-will despite the clamorous lack of appreciation surrounding him; he's a good one, plain and simple – he means no-one any harm. Despite his strong sense of social responsibility and his perceptions of society's conditioning, Dickens also believed in good and evil – he believed there were truly good people, and truly bad ones. He loved every genuine virtue, and every kindness; he detested the many forms of cruelty, and he heaped every imaginable scorn upon hypocrisy and selfishness. He was incapable of indifference.

He prefers Wemmick to Jaggers; but toward Jaggers he shows less loathing than fear. Jaggers is too dangerous to despise. When I was a teenager, I thought that Jaggers was always washing his hands and digging with his penknife under his fingernails because of how morally reprehensible (how morally filthy-dirty) his clients were; it was a case of the lawyer trying to rid his body of the contamination contracted by his proximity to the criminal element. I think now that this is only partially why Jaggers can never be, entirely, clean; I am far more certain that the filth Jaggers accumulates in his work is dirt from the work of the law itself – it is his *own* profession's crud that clings to him. This is why Wemmick is more human than Jaggers; it strikes Pip that Wemmick walks 'among the prisoners much as a gardener might walk among his plants' – yet Wemmick is capable of having his 'Walworth sentiments'; when he's at home with his 'aged parent', Wemmick is a sweetheart. The contamination is more permanently with Jaggers; his home is nearly as businesslike as his office, and the presence of his housekeeper, Molly – who is surely a murderess, spared the gallows *not* because she was innocent but because Jaggers got her off – casts the prison aura of Newgate over Jaggers's dinner table.

Of course, there are things to learn from Jaggers: the

attention he pays to that dull villain Drummle helps to open Pip's eyes to the unjust ways of the world – the world's standard of values is based on money and class, and on the assured success of brute aggressiveness. Through his hatred of Drummle, Pip also learns a little about himself – 'our worst weaknesses and meannesses are usually committed for the sake of the people whom we most despise,' he observes. We might characterize Pip's progress in the novel as the autobiography of a slow learner. He thinks he has grasped who Pumblechook is, right from the start; but the *degree* of Pumblechook's hypocrisy, his fawning, his dishonesty, and his false loyalty – based on one's station in life and revised, instantly, upon one's turn of fortune – is a continuing surprise and an education. Pumblechook is a strong minor character, a good man to hate. Missing – from our contemporary literature – is both the ability to praise as Dickens could praise (without reservation), and to hate as he could hate (completely). Is it our timorousness, or that the sociologist's and psychologist's more complicated view of villainy has removed from our literature not only absolute villains but absolute heroes?

Dickens had a unique affection for his characters, even for most of his villains. 'The bores in his books are brighter than the wits in other books,' Chesterton observes. 'Two primary dispositions of Dickens, to make the flesh creep and to make the sides ache, were . . . twins of his spirit,' Chesterton writes. Indeed, it was Dickens's love of the theatrical that made each of his characters – in his view – a *performer*. Because they were all actors, and therefore they were all important, all of Dickens's characters behave dramatically – and heroes and villains alike are given memorable qualities.

217

Magwitch is my hero, and what is most exciting and visceral in the story of *Great Expectations* concerns this convict who risks his life to see how his creation has turned out. How like Dickens that Magwitch is spared the real answer; his creation has not turned out very well. And what a story Magwitch's story is! It is Magwitch who enlivens the book's dramatic beginning; an escaped convict, he frightens a small boy into providing food for his stomach and a file for his leg-iron; and by returning to London, a hunted man, Magwitch not only contributes to the book's dramatic conclusion; he as effectively destroys Pip's expectations as he has created them. It is also Magwitch who provides us with the missing link in the story of Miss Havisham's jilting – he is our means for knowing who Estella is.

In 'the ruined garden' of Satis House, the rank weeds pollute a beauty that might have been; the rotting wedding cake is overrun with spiders and mice. Pip can never rid himself (or Estella, by association) of that prison 'taint'. The connection with crime that young Pip so inexplicably feels at key times in his courtship of Estella is, of course, foreshadowing the revelation that Pip is more associated with the convict Abel Magwitch than he knows. There is little humor remaining in Pip upon the discovery of his true circumstances. Even as a maltreated child, Pip is capable of exhibiting humor (at least, in remembrance); he recalls he was 'regaled with the scaly tips of the drumsticks of the fowls, and with those obscure corners of pork of which the pig, when living, had had the least reason to be vain'. But there is sparse wit in Dickens's language after Pip discovers who his benefactor is. The language itself grows thinner as the plot begins to race.

Both in the lushness of his language, when Dickens means to be lush, and in how spare he can be when he simply wants you to follow the story, he is ever conscious of his readers. It was relatively late in his life that he began to give public readings, yet his language was consistently written to be read aloud – the use of repetition, of refrains; the rich, descriptive lists that accompany a newly introduced character or place, the abundance of punctuation. Dickens overpunctuates; he makes long and potentially difficult sentences slower but easier to read – as if his punctuation is a form of stage direction, when reading aloud; or as if he is aware that many of his readers were reading his novels in serial form and needed nearly constant reminding. He is overly clear. He is a master of that device for making short sentences seem long, and long sentences readable – the semicolon! Dickens never wants a reader to be lost; but, at the same time, he never wants a reader to *skim*. It is rather hard going to skim Dickens; you will miss too much to make sense of anything. He made every sentence easy to read because he wanted you to read every sentence.

Imagine missing this parenthetical aside about marriage: 'I may here remark that I suppose myself to be better acquainted than any living authority with the ridgy effect of a wedding ring passing unsympathetically over the human countenance.' Of course, young Pip is referring to having his face scrubbed by his sister, but for the careful reader this is a reference to the general discomfort of marriage. And who cannot imagine that Dickens's own exhaustion and humiliation in the blacking warehouse informed Pip's sensitivity to his dull labors in the blacksmith's shop? 'In the little world in which children have their existence . . . there is nothing so finely perceived and so finely felt as injustice.' For 'injustice' was always Dickens's subject – and his broadest anger toward it is directed at injustice to children. It is both the sensitivity of a child and the vulnerability of an author in late middle-age (with the conviction that most of his happiness is behind him, and that most of his loneliness is ahead of him) that enhance young Pip's view of the marshes at night. 'I looked at the stars, and considered how awful it would be for a man to turn his face up to them as he froze to death, and see no help or pity in all the glittering multitude.'

Images of such brilliance are as enchanting in *Great Expectations* as its great characters and its humbling story. Dickens was a witness of a world moving at a great pace toward more powerful and less human institutions; he saw the outcasts of society's greed and hurry. 'In a passion of glorious violence,' Johnson writes, 'he defended the golden mean.' He believed that in order to defend the dignity of man it was necessary to uphold and cherish the individual.

When Dickens first finished *Great Expectations*, he was already running out of time; he was already exhausted. He would write only one more novel *(Our Mutual Friend*, 1864–5); *The Mystery of Edwin Drood* was never completed. He worked a full day on that last book the day he was stricken. Here is the final sentence he wrote: 'The cold stone tombs of centuries ago grow warm; and flecks of brightness dart into the sternest marble corners of the building, fluttering like wings.' Later, he tried a few letters; in one of them, Johnson tells us, he quoted Friar Laurence's warning to Romeo: 'These violent delights have violent ends.' Perhaps this was a premonition; in his novels, he exhibited a great fondness for premonitions.

Charles Dickens died of a paralytic stroke on a warm June evening in 1870; at his death, his eyes were closed but a tear was observed on his right cheek; he was fifty-eight. He lay in an open grave in Westminster Abbey for three days – there were so many thousands of mourners who came to pay their respects to the former child-laborer whose toil had once seemed so menial in the blacking warehouse at Hungerford Stairs.

# THE 158lb MARRIAGE
## John Irving

Severin Winter is not a man to take things lightly. His loving, like his wrestling, is decidedly heavyweight . . . a fact not lost on Utch, a lovely Viennese lady whose husband is rather taken (literally) by the delicate Edith, Severin's underweight wife. A bizarre *ménage à quatre* is the result of these convoluted desires as Irving blends farce and tragedy in another bubbling, brilliant novel.

'IRVING'S TALENT FOR STORYTELLING IS SO BRIGHT AND STRONG THAT HE GETS DOWN TO THE TRUTH OF HIS TIME'
*New York Times Book Review*

0 552 99208 9

# THE WORLD ACCORDING TO GARP
## John Irving

'IT IS NOT EASY TO FIND WORDS IN WHICH TO CONVEY THE JOY, THE EXCITEMENT, THE PASSION THIS SUPERB NOVEL EVOKES. THE IMAGINATION SOARS AS IRVING DRAWS US ON INEXORABLY INTO GARP'S WORLD, WHICH IS AT ONCE LARGER THAN LIFE AND AS REAL AS OUR OWN MOST PRIVATE DREAMS OF LIFE AND DEATH, LOVE, LUST AND FEAR . . . SOME OF THE MOST COLOURFUL CHARACTERS IN RECENT FICTION'
*Publishers Weekly*

'LIKE ALL GREAT WORKS OF ART, IRVING'S NOVEL SEEMS ALWAYS TO HAVE BEEN THERE, A DIAMOND SLEEPING IN THE DARK, CHIPPED OUT AT LAST FOR OUR ENRICHMENT AND DELIGHT . . . AS APPROACHABLE AS IT IS BRILLIANT, *GARP* PULSES WITH VITAL ENERGY'
*Cosmopolitan*

0 552 99205 4

**BLACK SWAN**

# THE HOTEL NEW HAMPSHIRE
## John Irving

John Irving's new novel – a hilarious family history with its own mythology and wisdom – takes its place alongside the great post-war American novels: *Catch-22*, *Slaughterhouse Five* and Irving's own *The World According to Garp*.

'AS GOOD AS, IF NOT BETTER THAN, *GARP*'
*Literary Review*

'A STARTLINGLY ORIGINAL FAMILY SAGA THAT COMBINES MACABRE HUMOUR WITH DICKENSIAN SENTIMENT AND OUTRAGE AT CRUELTY, DOGMATISM AND INJUSTICE . . . IRVING'S POPULARITY IS NOT HARD TO UNDERSTAND. HIS WORLD REALLY IS THE WORLD ACCORDING TO EVERYONE'
*Time*

0 552 99209 7

# A PRAYER FOR OWEN MEANY
## John Irving

'HIS BOOKS HAVE DONE FOR YOUNG PEOPLE NOW WHAT *CATCHER IN THE RYE* DID FOR YOUNG PEOPLE IN THE FIFTIES'
*Sunday Times*

In the summer of 1953, two eleven-year-old boys are playing in a Little League baseball game in Gravesend, New Hampshire; one of the boys, Owen Meany, hits a foul ball and kills his best friend's mother. Owen doesn't believe in accidents; he believes his is God's instrument. What happens to Owen after that 1953 foul is extraordinary and terrifying. At moments a comic, self-deluded victim, but in the end the principal, tragic actor in a divine plan, Owen Meany is the most heartbreaking hero John Irving has yet created.

0 552 99369 7

**BLACK SWAN**

# A SELECTION OF FINE WRITING
# AVAILABLE FROM BLACK SWAN

THE PRICES SHOWN BELOW WERE CORRECT AT THE TIME OF GOING TO PRESS.
HOWEVER TRANSWORLD PUBLISHERS RESERVE THE RIGHT TO SHOW NEW RETAIL
PRICES ON COVERS WHICH MAY DIFFER FROM THOSE PREVIOUSLY ADVERTISED IN
THE TEXT OR ELSEWHERE.

| | | | | |
|---|---|---|---|---|
| ❐ | 99550 9 | THE FAME HOTEL | Terence Blacker | £5.99 |
| ❐ | 99531 2 | AFTER THE HOLE | Guy Burt | £4.99 |
| ❐ | 99348 4 | SUCKING SHERBET LEMONS | Michael Carson | £5.99 |
| ❐ | 99465 0 | STRIPPING PENGUINS BARE | Michael Carson | £5.99 |
| ❐ | 99524 X | YANKING UP THE YO-YO | Michael Carson | £5.99 |
| ❐ | 99466 9 | A SMOKING DOT IN THE DISTANCE | Ivor Gould | £6.99 |
| ❐ | 99487 1 | JIZZ | John Hart | £5.99 |
| ❐ | 99169 4 | GOD KNOWS | Joseph Heller | £6.99 |
| ❐ | 99195 3 | CATCH 22 | Joseph Heller | £6.99 |
| ❐ | 99409 X | SOMETHING HAPPENED | Joseph Heller | £5.99 |
| ❐ | 99538 X | GOOD AS GOLD | Joseph Heller | £6.99 |
| ❐ | 99208 9 | THE 158LB MARRIAGE | John Irving | £5.99 |
| ❐ | 99204 6 | THE CIDER HOUSE RULES | John Irving | £6.99 |
| ❐ | 99209 7 | THE HOTEL NEW HAMPSHIRE | John Irving | £6.99 |
| ❐ | 99369 7 | A PRAYER FOR OWEN MEANY | John Irving | £6.99 |
| ❐ | 99206 2 | SETTING FREE THE BEARS | John Irving | £5.99 |
| ❐ | 99207 0 | THE WATER-METHOD MAN | John Irving | £6.99 |
| ❐ | 99205 4 | THE WORLD ACCORDING TO GARP | John Irving | £6.99 |
| ❐ | 99141 4 | PEEPING TOM | Howard Jacobson | £5.99 |
| ❐ | 99252 6 | REDBACK | Howard Jacobson | £5.99 |
| ❐ | 99567 3 | SAILOR SONG | Ken Kesey | £6.99 |
| ❐ | 99037 X | BEING THERE | Jerzy Kosinski | £3.99 |
| ❐ | 99552 5 | TALES OF THE CITY | Armistead Maupin | £5.99 |
| ❐ | 99086 8 | MORE TALES OF THE CITY | Armistead Maupin | £5.99 |
| ❐ | 99374 3 | SURE OF YOU | Armistead Maupin | £5.99 |
| ❐ | 99500 2 | THE RUINS OF TIME | Ben Woolfenden | £4.99 |

All Black Swan Books are available at your bookshop or newsagent, or can be ordered
from the following address:
Black Swan Books
Cash Sales Department
P.O. Box 11, Falmouth, Cornwall TR10 9EN

UK and B.F.P.O. customers please send a cheque or postal order (no currency) and allow
£1.00 for postage and packing for the first book plus 50p for the second book and 30p
for each additional book to a maximum charge of £3.00 (7 books plus).

Overseas customers, including Eire, please allow £2.00 for postage and packing for the first
book plus £1.00 for the second book and 50p for each subsequent title ordered.

NAME (Block letters) ........................................................................................................................

ADDRESS ...........................................................................................................................................